# JEWELS

## The Town Hall Meeting

Darrius Jerome Gourdine

# DJG

# Enterprises

Photography: James McDuff

Cover and Promotional Graphic Design: Jossan Robinson

Book Layout and Website Design: Norman Rich, Lighthouse Strategic Group

For book signings and speaking engagements, send all inquiries to darrius@jewels1906.com.

www.jewels1906.com

ISBN: 0-9755660-4-6

# DEDICATION

This book is dedicated to my son Dylan Joshua Gourdine who I hope to one day enter the House of Alpha if it be his desire.

# THE SEVEN JEWELS
# THE FOUNDERS OF ALPHA PHI ALPHA FRATERNITY

Jewel Henry Arthur Callis

Jewel Charles Henry Chapman

Jewel Eugene Kinckle Jones

Jewel George Biddle Kelley

Jewel Nathaniel Allison Murray

Jewel Robert Harold Ogle

Jewel Vertner Woodson Tandy

# JEWELS:
# THE TOWN HALL MEETING

*featuring...*

Howard Franklin, *Past Sargent-At-Arms,
Omicron Lambda Alpha Chapter*

Sean Christopher Gayle, *Past President, Kappa Xi
Lambda Chapter (The Wall Street Alphas)*

Darrius Jerome Gourdine, *Author*

Robert L. Harris Jr., *Alpha Phi Alpha National
Historian*

Denny N. Johnson, *Alpha Phi Alpha's Director of
Membership Services*

Kagi Kananga, *Alpha Phi Alpha's Western Regional
Assistant Vice President*

William Douglass Lyle, *Alpha Phi Alpha's
Executive Director*

Darryl R. Matthews Sr., *Alpha Phi Alpha's 32nd General
President*

Sean L. McCaskill, *Alpha Phi Alpha's Past Eastern
Regional Vice President*

Gregory Parks, *Law Professor, Educator, Author*

Donald Ross, *Alpha Phi Alpha Historical Commission*

Julian Wilson, *Grandson of Jewel Robert Harold Ogle*

I woke up this morning and literally pinched myself. I actually took two fingers, put them against my arm, and pinched myself. It's not every day that one gets a chance to moderate an open forum discussion between men that he respects and men who he considers heroes. The founders of Alpha Phi Alpha Fraternity; the Seven Jewels, are heroes to me and hundreds of thousands of other members and admirers of the fraternity. What once was an idea and a literary society transformed into an organization whose members are some of the most brilliant minds of the Black race. The common expression shared amongst members of the fraternity which states There Goes An Alpha Man can be uttered with confidence if one examines leaders in any organization or industry. Whether the industry is academia, sports, religion, politics, government, law, civic service, private business, medicine, progressive thought or grassroots community development, brothers of Alpha Phi Alpha stand in leadership positions.

I remember when I first came into contact with Alpha Phi Alpha. As a kid growing up in New Jersey in the 70's and 80's, I had never seen fraternities. The Black Greek letter organization culture was not as widespread and mainstream as it is now. There wasn't social media or technology which are every day necessities today. There were no high school step teams as stepping was an art form reserved for members of fraternities and sororities only. I attended an all-boys high school in East Orange, NJ and had never seen any semblance of Greek life. I went to college with the notion that I would never pledge because my only exposure was being told that fraternities do embarrassing things to pledges and I wanted none of that. I then saw a classmate in college go through drastic changes which ranged from his sudden bald head to drab clothing which he wore every day. He also walked in straight lines only and fell asleep in class almost daily. I didn't know him well enough to speak to him or ask him why he was walking funny so I simply observed him from afar. It wasn't for another two weeks after he caught my attention that I saw him on the main campus marching in formation with his line brothers. I quickly ran to get a glimpse at what I would soon learn were the Sphinxmen. These men were pledging Alpha Phi Alpha Fraternity and had to march in line bunched together. This produced one sound, even though seven of them were marching together. They were chanting words as they marched and I noticed a bunch of guys walking with them. Each of the guys around them wore fraternity jackets. The jackets were black with the letters A Phi A on the front. On the back were names and a number. I saw names like Atum Ra, The Boy Tutt, Rhapsody in Black, The Juggernaut, Prime Minister and Ice Man. I didn't know what any of it was but it caught my attention and intrigued me.

I remember running into my roommate while boarding the shuttle bus to the dorm. "Hey man! Where you been? Did you see the guys marching and singing or whatever?"

"What?"

"The guys! They had on khaki pants and black hoodies and the boots! They had on black boots! And then the frat guys were walking with them! You didn't see it?"

"Oh the Alphas. Nah I missed it! Where were they?"

"Right in front of the library but then they went down past the chapel and right into the Engineering building! They had a crowd following them!"

"Yeah that's the Alphas. The guys that are the pledgees are called Sphinxmen. They're gonna be Alphas soon if they can make it through."

I didn't know what Alpha Phi Alpha or the term Sphinxman meant. Since I love to read and research things that I don't know, I went to the library on campus to look up Alpha Phi Alpha. Little did I know that the library at Howard University is an archive of information on Black culture. The library holds every magazine ever published by the fraternity from the early days at Cornell University to the present day. I was able to begin to read from the early days of the fraternity as the organization had its genesis. The very campus that I sat and read in became the second chapter for the fraternity and I was honored to be seated on hallowed ground. I read that the first general president of the fraternity was a Howard University student. I was impressed by the accomplishments of the chapter and I wasn't even a member. I turned page after page and magazine after magazine reading of the early years of Alpha. So many accomplishments in expanding the organization and maintaining its infant stability.

I arrive at the magazines dated in the 1920's. I'd read a decade and a half of the first years of Alpha Phi Alpha and I am blown away. I had never seen so many accomplishments from Black men in my life. I was both overwhelmed and speechless. Then one particular Sphinx magazine literally made me gasp when I saw the cover. On the cover was a man who I recognized immediately.

When I was a senior in high school, my church sponsored a graduation luncheon for the seniors. It was at a nice facility with a keynote speaker. I don't remember one word the keynote speaker said. He was rather boring in my opinion. Nothing he said that afternoon left any impression upon me. After the event, each of the graduates had an opportunity to meet him and shake his hand. I approached him with my parents, my brother and sister. He was a nice gentleman with a warm smile. He had gray hair and a firm handshake indicative of a much younger man. He pushed his glasses up his nose as I let his hand go. He had a deep voice and he got right to the point when he asked questions.

"What college will you be attending in the fall young man?"

"I'm going to Howard University in Washington." I replied proudly.

"Really? My grandson Randy is going to Howard! You should come to my house and meet him!"

I didn't want to go to his house. He had bored me to death in his speech so I had no interest in going to his home nor in meeting his grandson. My father on the other hand was extremely excited to meet him and be invited to his home. Within a week, my entire family was driving to his home in New Jersey. We lived in East Orange, NJ and he didn't live too far away from us. My brother and sister were occupied with pushing each other next to me in the back seat so I stared out the window and dreaded this evening of boringness I was about to endure.

We arrived at his house and his wife opened the door for us. She was very nice like everybody's grandmother. She sat us in their living room just as he came out to greet us. He flashed the warm smile once again and welcomed us into his home. The first thing I noticed about his home were the pictures on his walls. He had a picture of himself standing next to President Ronald Reagan. That one caught my attention first. I scanned the wall to the next picture and it was of him and Dr. Martin Luther King Jr. They were shaking hands in the photo. The next picture I saw was he and Malcolm X. I look back at him with a surprised look on my face. I now want to know who this man is. I still didn't know who he was, even though his bio was in the graduation luncheon program I tossed under my bed at home.

For the next few hours, he tells my captivated family of his experiences covering the current events of the world. He was a journalist who covered the Cuban Missile crisis. Larger than that for me though was that he told us that Jackie Robinson complained about the lack of Black journalists since ABC had no Blacks covering his baseball career. That was a boost in this man's career. He opened the door to several Black journalists and told us about interviewing both Martin and Malcolm. One story after another. Each more captivating than the next. This man had me hanging on every word and I was in awe. I left his home that evening with two things; a newfound respect for him and his name... Mr. Mal Goode.

Now, two years later, I am in the Moorland Spingarn Research Center in the Howard University library with an old Sphinx magazine in my hand. On the cover of the magazine is Mal Goode. I hadn't spoken to him or even thought of him since I left his home that evening but I remembered immediately who he was. I also remember that he gave me his phone number and instructed me to call him if I ever needed anything. I ran from the library back to my dorm to try and find his number in my heap of belongings.

I found his number and called him. This was before cell phones so I called his home number. He answered.

"Mr. Goode! You probably don't remember me but my name is Darrius Gourdine. I am a Howard University student and I started college with your grandson Randy."

"Oh yes! Darrius Gourdine from New Jersey! How are you son?"

"I'm fine sir, how are you?"

"Fine. How are things in school down there at Howard?"

"Things are great. I'm doing well. I have a question for you sir. I'm reading a magazine for Alpha Phi Alpha Fraternity Incorporated and I see your picture on the cover. Are you a member of Alpha Phi Alpha Fraternity Incorporated?"

His voice indicated a smile, as if one can tell if someone is smiling by the sound of their voice. "I became a member at the University of Pittsburgh. I sang the fraternity hymn with all seven jewels. I'm a proud and active brother of Alpha Phi Alpha. I covered my brother Martin King's funeral. Yes I'm a proud brother!"

For the next hour, Mal Goode told me stories of his interactions with his fraternity brothers of Alpha Phi Alpha. I listened in amazement to the man who I was bored by two years prior yet captivated by now. Clearly a storyteller, Mr. Goode told me of this brother or that brother. One was a CEO and another was a popular reverend. One was a sports legend while another was a politician. All brothers of Alpha Phi Alpha and all seemingly friends of his.

As we hung up the phone, I knew that I wanted to be a member of his fraternity. I knew without a shadow of a doubt that I wanted to become a friend through fraternity affiliation. I wanted to find out all that I could about Alpha Phi Alpha. I wanted to find out why that classmate wore the same clothes every day and walked in straight lines. I wanted to research the founders of the fraternity and find out what drove them to create the fraternity... the first fraternity for Black students. I wanted to become an Alpha.

Now I stand over two decades later as a brother. I stand as a member of Alpha Phi Alpha. I remember the conversation that I had with Brother Mal Goode once I was on line and had become a Sphinxman. His words of encouragement helped me along in my journey toward membership. I thanked him for igniting the fire that still burns inside of me for the brotherhood of Alpha.

Today I pinch myself and recollect my journey into Alpha as the event that will transpire today is probably one of the more significant events in Alpha Phi Alpha's amazing history. I have the awesome task of moderating an open discussion between the founding Jewels of Alpha Phi Alpha and various members of the brotherhood today. What an awesome conversation this is going to be! I've anticipated the questions that may come up and the answers that may go back and forth. What an incredible opportunity to converse with the fathers of the brotherhood that you belong to? If this brotherhood means anything to anyone then this conversation will be everything to everyone.

When the opportunity presented itself to moderate the Town Hall discussion between the fraternity's beloved founders and current brothers, I jumped at the chance. What better venue than the house on East State Street in Ithaca, NY. 411 East State Street was the meeting place and the holder of many of the earliest conversations about the brotherhood that exists today. Countless number of lives have been touched, changed, mentored and bettered because of the meetings in 411. A sense of nostalgia as well as wonderment will fill the room before questions begin to fly back and forth between the Alpha brothers. It's surreal to imagine and impossible to put into words. I wonder who will be the first to open the discussion. Will one of the Jewels be first? Nathaniel Allison Murray. George Biddle Kelley. Vertner Woodson Tandy. Will one of the current brothers step forward with a question or statement? Gregory Parks? Sean Christopher Gayle? Howard Franklin?

I glance at my phone to check the time and realize it's almost Game Time. Brother arrival times are approaching. I walk into the kitchen area to check on the food. Broiled lamb chops. Peas in a tub. Lady fingers. Many of the menu items that the brothers shared in this house or memorized by learning the history will be feasted upon today. I'm sure many of the things that we embraced as gentlemen interested in Alpha Phi Alpha will be stirred within us as we sit and dialogue with the founders.

I look at my phone again, this time not to check the time but to see who is calling. I answer.

"Bruh"

"Bruh!" Sean says. Sean Gayle and I have greeted each other in this manner for as long as I've known him. Sean is both an intellectual and a great spiritual mind. He's perfect for the discussion with the Jewels today as he is a brother's brother and a leader amongst many. I've had the good pleasure of watching Sean grow up in Alpha from his earliest days as a neophyte to his days as the president of one of the premier chapters in the Eastern Regional, Kappa Xi Lambda (the Wall Street Alphas).

"How far away are you?" I ask.

"I'm pulling up. Probably two or three minutes away."

"What? Why you so early?"

"Bruh, I'm about to talk to the Jewels! You lucky I didn't show up and sleep out front on the sidewalk!"

I laugh and realize he's right. This is historic and we're all excited. Now I'm surprised more brothers aren't arriving early as Sean is.

"Are any of them there yet?"

"No. Not yet." I respond. "Who you looking forward to talking to most? I ask.

"I have an affinity for each of them for different reasons. I mean, Jewel Eugene Kinckle Jones because of his contribution to Beta Chapter. I like Jewel Tandy, he appears to be a nerd."

"Yeah you are kinda nerdy bruh!" I say laughing.

"Shut up! I hate bros!"

We both laugh. Sean continues. "I like Ogle because

he was married at a young age and made it work. I like Callis because he was around the longest. So I like them all, just different reasons."

"I hear ya. Aight let me go. Still making sure I'm ready."

"You'll do fine D. You been preparing your whole Alpha life for this."

I smile. "Thanks man. See ya in a minute."

We end the call and I take one final sweep of the room. Chairs set up for the brothers. A panel style set up for the Jewels. A podium for me although I want this to be a lot less formal. I want to encourage the brothers to open up and ask whatever they want related to the fraternity. I believe that will be the sentiment once the ice is broken. I think back to this room in the fall of 1905 and early 1906. The conversations between C.C. Poindexter and a young Henry Callis. Eugene Jones being introduced to the group in the fall of 1906 and being so influential that he was counted as one of the seven. So much history in one building and now history repeats itself as the past meeting the present.

The first knock on the door brings me from the past meeting the present to the present itself as I know Sean has arrived. I open the door and greet him with the fraternal handshake. Truer words were never written than '...men unacquainted, enter, shake hands and depart friends.' I've greeted Sean in this fashion for a number of years yet today's handshake is more firm, more fraternal. He smiles as he enters the house, the first to arrive.

The floodgate of arrivals soon open as Brother Denny Johnson, the fraternity's Director of Membership Services and Brother William Douglass Lyle, the fraternity's Executive Director and Chief Operating Officer have entered the house. They drove together since they both came from the fraternity's national headquarters in Baltimore.

"Brothers, if you want to start with some cheese and crackers, be my guest until all the brothers arrive." I offer as we wait on the brothers to arrive.

"I can't even think about eating!" Denny says. "I just can't wait to meet the Jewels and talk to them. I ain't gonna lie, this is gonna be epic."

The brothers seem to agree.

Brother Denny and Brother Wil speak to Sean as I tend to the door. Another knock and I assume it's Brother Howard Franklin and Brother McCaskill who I know travelled together. I step into the door which is already open and stop as I am now standing face to face with Nathaniel Allison Murray. We smile at each other and I try to say hello. I hear it in my head but nothing comes out of my mouth.

"Are any of the brothers here yet?" he asks directly.

"Uh yeah. You're Jewel Murray. Jewel Nathaniel Allison Murray."

He smiles. "Yes. And you are?" he extends his hand

toward me.

"Darrius... I mean, Brother Gourdine. Brother Darrius Jerome Gourdine."

"Good to meet you Brother Gourdine." As Nathaniel Allison Murray passes me, I think about what I know of him. What I remember from my days of learning the founders. The countless hours I spent memorizing their names and occupations as was the criteria for membership. Jewel Nathaniel Allison Murray is from Washington DC and is one of the two Jewel founders to charter Beta Chapter at Howard University. This has always been intriguing to me as I know he attended the prestigious M School in DC for high school. This proved to be a significant piece of history as many of the charter members of Beta Chapter also attended the M School. A person would be lead to deduce that he had a strong hand to play in the men who were selected to be the charter brothers of Beta Chapter. Did he perhaps handpick those students personally? Did he personally reach out to certain brothers but not to others? Did the fact that his mother worked at Howard University have any bearing on him choosing Howard for Beta Chapter? Did the fact that his mother worked at Howard University have any bearing on him not attending Howard but going to Cornell instead? I've personally wondered about some of these things for years. Guess I can just ask him now.

One by one, brothers arrive intermingled with founders. Jewel George Biddle Kelley ironically arrives with Jewel Vertner Woodson Tandy. I say their arrival is ironic because their personalities seem to oppose one another. One serious, one jovial. One to the point, one beating around the bush. One looking to make a serious point, one looking to make a serious joke. Both come in smiling as they re-enter the house they know so well.

Jewel Eugene Kinckle Jones seems to be in a deep discussion with Brother Bob Harris and Brother Gregory Parks. What a joining of minds between the three! Brilliant minds, each in their own right. Brother Gregory Parks is the author of several books including Alpha Phi Alpha: A Legacy of Greatness, The Demands of Transcendence and Leadership & Service: The Making and Remaking of Alpha Phi Alpha. He is a well-respected professor and has done numerous studies on Black Greek culture in its many aspects. He is by far the leading expert on Black Greek Letter Organizations and hazing in this country. His works are well documented and widely read. Brother Robert "Bob" Harris Jr. is the national historian for the fraternity and a unique voice of leadership within Alpha Phi Alpha. His commitment to the preservation of the fraternity's history is impressive to say the least. Brother Harris makes the connection for African Americans between their history and the current cultural, socioeconomic and political positions we find ourselves in. He is a man of genius intellect and has authored more than 40 articles and chapters in academic journals and books. The mere fact that Brother Parks and Brother Harris have gravitated to Jewel Jones is special.

I look over the room of brothers. Alpha men. From different walks of life. A variety of backgrounds, occupations, and stories. These men represent a lifespan of opinions and perspectives. Since the span of years in the fraternity is decades between the current brothers and the Jewel founders, the conversation today should be interesting to say the least. All of the founders are here except Jewel Robert Harold Ogle who hasn't arrived yet. Each of the brothers is conversing with I suppose the founder of his choice. Each brother is in his own separate world, enjoying the conversations. I've asked brothers not to ask the founders the questions we have reserved for the Town Hall meeting as to not spoil the answers or have to have the founders repeat what they have already said.

The next brother to arrive is a college brother. His name is Kagi Kananga. He is the youngest brother attending the Town Hall Meeting and has traveled the furthest. I exchange greetings with him as soon as he walks in the door. "Brother Kananga. So glad you're here bro! Come on in."

"I'm so happy to be here, I wouldn't miss this for the world Brother Gourdine!" He says with an excited sound to his voice and wide open eyes.

I turn to introduce him to some of the brothers. "Sean, bruh this is Brother Kagi, the college brother that will be with us for the meeting. Kagi this is Sean Gayle. We're both from Beta Chapter and Sean is a past president and dean for the Wall Street Alphas in New York."

"Oh what's up bro! Good to meet you!"

"Likewise brother!" Sean says as he and Kagi exchange handshakes.

The Jewels Town Hall Meeting won't begin until all invited brothers are in attendance and we are still awaiting a few. One Jewel founder and three invited brothers. Most of the food that has been displayed hasn't been eaten as I'm sure the brothers are much too excited to eat and would rather spend this time talking to one another. Becoming familiar with a person that you have intimately studied as each of us has studied the Jewels is absolutely mind blowing. I look forward to this conversation being enlightening and thought provoking. Alpha Phi Alpha has assembled some of the greatest minds of the past 100 plus years. Bridging the gap of time and bringing those minds together is a feat no one has ever witnessed or imagined.

Brother Donald Ross enters the house. There aren't many Alpha men today who have the extensive knowledge of the history of Alpha Phi Alpha than Brother Donald Ross. He's a perfect brother to be in attendance for The Town Hall Meeting. I'm sure he will be knowledgeable of many of the things that the Jewels may mention and can comment further than any of us. Always pleasant, he and I greet one another in the manner of the brotherhood.

Then I hear my voice called. "Brother Gourdine! How the hell are ya!"

I turn back to the door to that familiar voice. Before

I see who is speaking, I know by the sound of the voice who it is. With open arms, Brother Howard Kingphish Franklin is standing behind me as he has just entered the house. He travelled with Brother Sean McCaskill and they are both smiling as they enter. Howard greets me with a hug before we exchange the fraternal handshake.

"Kingphish! What's up bro!"

"Man it's good to be here!" Howard looks around the room and then looks back at me. "Yeah bruh, it's good to be here! Where's Jewel George Biddle Kelley?" Howard is loud. Extremely loud. Anyone that has ever met Brother Franklin knows that his voice or laughter will fill a room. He is a gifted musician which brings him incredible balance. I've watched him play several events and the calming aspect of him as a musician is the complete opposite of the raging passion he is as a man. Howard will get in a brother's face and tell that brother what he thinks without holding back. Howard will then embrace the same brother and let him know that it is only the love of Alpha that drives him the way that he is driven. The entire room has turned our direction as Howard has asked for Jewel Kelley in loud Howard fashion.

"I'm here brother." Jewel Kelley responds. Jewel Kelley is standing with Jewel Callis and Brother Darryl R. Matthews Sr. Jewel Callis is Alpha Phi Alpha's 6th General President and Brother Matthews is Alpha Phi Alpha's 32nd General President. All 3 are looking at myself, Howard and Sean McCaskill as we stand by the door. They along with all the brothers in the room await Howard's next statement... as most do when it comes to good brother Howard.

"Jewel Big Brother George Biddle Kelley it is a pleasure and an honor to meet you!" Howard says as he approaches Jewel Kelley. Both hands are extended to take Jewel Kelley's hands and Howard is almost bent over out of sheer respect. As they take hold of each other's hands, a powerful thing is witnessed. Although every brother in the room has already extended greetings and the fraternal handshake with one another, there's something about the entire room watching Jewel George Biddle Kelley and Brother Howard Franklin embrace. This is a coming together of sorts of the old and new yet the similar mentality of these two men is astonishing. All of us know the personalities of both these brothers. Jewel Kelley because we studied him and Howard because we know him. Each are fiery brothers that will never back down from their position. Each are passionate about the things they hold dear and the truth that they believe. Each hold and maintain strong convictions that are unwavering. Each has been in a position within Alpha Phi Alpha where they may not have been but liked they were always respected. This is a coming together indeed and the entire reason behind The Jewels Town Hall. It is absolute time for a reflection of our history and to hear the voices of those that created this. At the same time, it is time for us to create new dialogue and approach the issues facing each brother, our community, our race and

Black men overall. Mentorship, civic responsibility, financial independence, and servanthood is the order of the day and this day we shall seize and transcend. This is the power of this connection bridging old and young, past and present.

Howard continues. "You're the Jewel I have admired the most as I've been told that I'm most like you. I might kick the door in at a chapter meeting you know!"

"I've been known to turn over a chair or two." Jewel Kelley says.

"Or three!" Jewel Vertner Tandy blurts out loudly. Everyone in the room laughs.

I'm already overjoyed at the sentiment in the room. Brothers unacquainted yet very much in the know of one another. Meeting familiar souls for the first time. What an experience. What a powerful treasure we have within our ranks. The House of Alpha is indeed all that is spoken about it and I can't wait to begin the conversation.

As Howard settles in and continues to talk to Jewel Kelley, a pair of brothers knock yet enter the house without me opening the door. Of all the brothers in attendance, both Jewel founders and brothers in attendance, this pair is probably the pair that most have been waiting to see together. How appropriate that they arrive together and enter the house together! These two are not only bonded by the brotherhood that is Alpha Phi Alpha but they are also bonded by blood. Brother Julian Wilson is a well-respected brother of Alpha based on his love for the fraternity and his fellowship amongst the brothers. He is also widely known as the grandson of Jewel Robert Harold Ogle. They have walked into the home together.

"Bob." Jewel Callis says with a smile.

"Henry. Good to see you brother." The two old friends embrace with a hug before exchanging the fraternal handshake. It's always a pleasure to share friendship with the brothers. With an organization as large as most fraternities are, the reality is that all members are not friends. It's good to have true friendship with the members. When you have that, you have no problem calling them brothers. "Henry I want you to meet Brother Julian. He's my grandson."

"Grandson! Pleasure to meet you good brother." Henry greets Julian.

"The pleasure is mine sir. Indeed it is." Julian responds as he exchanges handshakes with Jewel Brother Callis.

All brothers are here now and we are ready and prepared to begin.

"Brothers! Brothers! If I can have your attention please. We're now all here and ready to begin. I'm sure you guys are eager to get started with our discussions so if you could all take your seats, we can get started. Thank you."

Jewel Tandy loads a few more items onto his plate

before he takes his seat and everyone settles down. The original thought for the layout of this meeting was panel style where the Jewel founders would be on one side and the brothers on the other. Brother Denny Johnson, the fraternity's current Director of Membership Services suggested to me to do a more informal seating arrangement. I agreed wholeheartedly to ensure brothers are relaxed and ready to fully discuss as the true spirit of the fraternity moves them. The chairs are arranged in a circle but not as strict. There are a few that are out of place and a few of the founders had already sat down as the other brothers arrived. This is truly informal. I take my seat and everyone focuses on me to begin.

"Brothers, it is an honor to be here and to serve you in this capacity. Before we begin, I want to thank you all for agreeing to participate and I want to encourage you to open up and feel free to speak as you wish. As you all know, this is a once in a lifetime type of opportunity so please take full advantage of it."

"Oh we will good brother!" Brother McCaskill blurts out. Everyone laughs as he laughs as well. Sean is a good friend of mine as he and I pledged in the same semester of Spring 1990. Sean has served in several leadership positions in Alpha, most notably the Vice President of the Eastern Region. I laugh with my Sands and good friend Sean.

"The first thing we want to do is introduce ourselves. Obviously the Jewels need no introduction but I want to afford them the same opportunity we all have. So if each brother can one at a time give us your name, chapter and school or grad chapter of initiation, and a little something about yourselves. I'll start. My name is Darrius Jerome Gourdine and I am an initiate of Beta Chapter at Howard University. I crossed into Alpha in the spri..."

"Beta Chapter! Yes indeed! The chapter I founded!" Jewel Jones proclaims proudly.

"So what? I founded Alpha Chapter!" Jewel Vertner Woodson Tandy says immediately. Everyone laughs as do I. I see the Jewels got jokes.

"Brothers, if we can keep the side comments and conversations to a minimum until we at least get through all the introductions, that would be greatly appreciated." Jewel Charles Henry Chapman is a man of very few words. His speeches were always to the point. His serious nature complimented his persona and it seems the other founders are used to his demeanor. The room settles down and I continue.

"I was initiated at Beta Chapter in the spring of 1990. I've served the fraternity in the Alpha Gamma Lambda Chapter here in New York and the Omicron Lambda Alpha Chapter in DC. I was historian for OLA for four terms." I look to my right for Brother Donald Ross to continue.

"Brother Gourdine, if I may, before you continue." Jewel Murray interrupts. "I open each meeting with the Lord's prayer. Would the brothers indulge me once again?"

"Most certainly Jewel Murray. By all means." I say.

"Thank you. Brothers, if we may bow our heads. Our Father, who art in heaven, hallowed be thy name. Thy kingdom come, thy will be done on Earth as it is in heaven. Give us this day our daily bread, and forgive us our trespasses. As we forgive those, who..."

Most of the brothers are saying the prayer along with Jewel Murray. This is quite a sight. Men praying together is a powerful thing to witness. Alpha men pray together after every singing of the fraternal hymn. This event I am witnessing however is the opening of The Town Hall Meeting. It is beautiful that Jewel Murray opens this meeting in the same manner he opened every meeting as a member of Mu Lambda Chapter in Washington, DC.

"...trespass against us. And lead us not, into temptation but deliver us from evil. For thine is the kingdom, the power and the glory forever. Amen."

"Amen." The brothers respond in unison.

"Thank you brothers."

"No, thank you Jewel Murray. Brother Ross you can go now." I say.

"Greetings brothers, my name is Brother Donald Ross and I was initiated into the Beta Theta Chapter at Bluefield State College in Bluefield West Virginia. I made my entrance into Alpha on May 7, 1983. I wanted to become a brother because the Alphas that I had met at that time told me that I was Alpha material. The organization itself seemed decent enough and I was curious to see how I would handle the pledge process. I'm glad I made the decision to become and Alpha and I have become a student of the history of this illustrious organization since I've become a brother. Thank you so much for having me. I can't tell you what this means to me to be a part of this discussion." His pause indicates that he is finished.

"I guess I'm next. My name is Eugene Jones. Most of you know me as Jewel Eugene Kinckle Jones. Some of you know me as Kinckle. Either way, it's good to be known and respected. I was on the first initiate line here at Cornell in the fall of 1906. It was with earnest diligence that I founded this organization with these fine gentlemen. Seems like just yesterday Henry and I were discussing the name of our organization and assigning its meaning. Everything about Alpha Phi Alpha to me has been well orchestrated and calculated from the onset. Looking through the decades from the perspective of the early days, it's astonishing to me the levels of accomplishment we've attained. But let me stop here before I get too wordy. I'm sure I'll have ample time to elaborate on the state of the fraternity through the years."

Next is Brother Harris. "My name is Brother Robert Harris Jr. Most in the fraternity call me Bob. I am the national historian for the fraternity. I was initiated at Theta Chapter in Chicago in 1963. In 1975 I joined the faculty here at Cornell as an assistant professor of African American history at the Africana Studies and Research Center. I became the Director of the Center in 1986. I became special assistant to the provost in 1994. I was named vice provost for diversity and faculty development in 2000. One of my greatest accomplishments here at Cornell was in 2004 when I was promoted to full professor of African American history and later when I achieved the professor emeritus status."

"Greetings brothers my name is Gregory Parks and I was initiated in 1997 into the Mu Lambda Chapter in Washington DC."

"Yes! Mu Lambda Chapter! I remember it well." Jewel Ogle replies as he nods his head toward Jewel Murray who helped to charter Mu Lambda Chapter with him. Mu Lambda Chapter is one of the oldest and most respected of Alpha's graduate chapters. Founded by the two Washingtonian founders, the chapter has been known to house some of the oldest active brothers in Alpha.

Brother Parks continues. "Since becoming a brother, I've focused my attention on studying and researching Alpha as well as the other Black Greek letter organizations. I've learned and presented the many aspects, repercussions and pitfalls of hazing. I've probably become one of the leading authorities on hazing in this country."

"Don't be so modest!" Howard Franklin states.

Some of the brothers laugh. Not all. Brother Parks shoots Howard a glance with a smile but a posture as if to say "You're not funny... at all Howard."

"Some of my published works include African American Fraternities and Sororities: The Legacy and the Vision, Alpha Phi Alpha: A Legacy of Greatness, The Demands of Transcendence..."

"A Legacy of Greatness! I admire that!" Jewel Eugene Kinckle Jones says.

Gregory continues. "Thank you Jewel Jones! That means a lot. Matter fact, you have no idea how much it means that the title alone meets your approval. I've also written and published Black Greek Letter Organizations in the 21$^{st}$ Century, Invictus: Hazing and the Future of Black Greek-letter Organizations. I'm also very proud of my most recent book on Alpha, Leadership and Service: The Making and Remaking of Alpha Phi Alpha. I'm a law professor at Wake Forest University. I have an M.S. in Forensic Psychology from the City University of New York, an M.A. and Ph.D. in Clinical Psychology from the University of Kentucky and a J.D. from Cornell University."

"Impressive!" Jewel Tandy says.

"My scholarly books have been published with Oxford University Press, The New Press, the University Press of Kentucky, the University Press of Mississippi, and Fairleigh Dickinson University Press. My scholarly articles have appeared in the Indiana Law Journal, the Wake Forest Law Review, DePaul Law Review, Florida State University Law Review, Marquette Law Review, Villanova Law Review, Howard Law Journal, University of Pennsylvania Law Review, Cardozo Law Review de novo, and the Cornell Journal of Law and

Public Policy."

"Wow! Now there goes an Alpha man indeed!" Jewel Tandy says with a smile.

"Yeah, bruh got more degrees than a thermometer!" Howard says.

Jewel Henry Arthur Callis is next. "Let me just say that I am already very impressed with you brothers. Just hearing the list of the books that you've written Brother..."

"Parks. Gregory Parks."

"Yes, Brother Parks. Please excuse me as I try to learn and remember all of your names."

"That's quite alright!" Brother Parks says with a smile.

"Hearing the list of books and articles that Brother Gregory Parks has done warms my heart. This is what I envisioned when we founded this organization. I envisioned a group of intelligent Black men who would stand boldly at the forefront of progressive thought. Great job Brother Parks. I'm sure your work is impactful."

I look at Brother Parks who is smiling but I know is containing his true emotions. How must it feel to be told by a founder of Alpha Phi Alpha that he is proud of the Alpha that you are? This is a moment in time that I know none of us will forget. Especially Brother Parks.

"My name is Henry A. Callis. Founder of Alpha Phi Alpha and very pleased and honored to be here."

"My name is Charles Chapman. I became a brother well before December 4th, 1906. The steps that led us to fraternity, led us through brotherhood. This is what we attempted to extend well beyond the city limits of Ithaca. I believe we have succeeded. Thank you."

"I'm Nathaniel Murray, originally from Washington, DC. It's my pleasure to meet brothers that I have not had the pleasure of meeting prior to today. I look forward to our spirited dialogue. I look to learn from you as I believe we can all learn from one another."

"Brothers! Brothers! Brothers! My name is Howard Franklin! I was made right at the Double O... Omicron Omicron Chapter of Alpha Phi Alpha! I'm a proud Alpha man and I bleed this black and gold! I wanna say thank you from the bottom of my heart to these seven men! Without you all, we wouldn't be here. I've made a lot of friendships in the house. Everything we will ever need is in the house. I've probably made a good deal of enemies in the house too!"

Everyone laughs. Especially those of us that know Howard.

"But seriously, this thing is deep in my heart and I cherish it and I love it. Much respect to the seven Jewels. All of you. And that's real from me. Real talk. Thank you!"

"Good brothers my name is Brother Denny Johnson.

I am a 1989 initiate of the Delta Gamma Chapter seated proudly at Alabama A&M University. I am the 10th member of the line which is named Eleven Pieces of a Dream. I've been an active brother in the fraternity since I crossed. I was chapter president for the Omicron Lambda Alpha Chapter for 4 consecutive terms. I'm now the Director of Membership Services in the national office. My decision to seek membership into Alpha Phi Alpha Fraternity, Incorporated was based on three words: academics, brotherhood and service. Although I have an older brother who is 10 years my senior, I grew up during my pre-teen and adolescence years as an only child. Upon arriving on the campus of Alabama A&M University for the fall semester 1987, I had no knowledge of the fraternity other than the notoriety of them as the smart guys."

"Glad we're still known for our intellect and academic prowess!" Jewel Chapman states.

"C.C. would be proud!" Jewel Callis makes his comment as a joke yet there is truth in all comedy. C.C. Poindexter's passion was to ignite the students to create a literary society more geared toward academics than the brotherhood of a fraternity. The fact that Alphas are stereotyped as 'smart guys' proves to be an interesting dynamic based on our founding. On the one hand, we are typecast as overly intelligent. That is absolutely what C.C. would've wanted. On the other hand, we are a brotherhood ahead of brotherhoods. We are a fraternity in every aspect of the word. That is absolutely what C.C. didn't want.

Denny continues. "Well, as a scholar myself who wanted to make a difference in the community, while actually sharing a bond of brotherhood, I thrust myself to accomplish something that I didn't think I could. I especially didn't know if it was possible for me on an HBCU campus where the chapter was most popular throughout the region and nationwide. I did it however. I did. So happy that I did. So proud that I did. I've continued my commitment to the brotherhood as well as contributed humble service, while maintaining the creed to academic excellence. I reflect back to that chilly November Thanksgiving weekend in 1988 when I officially submitted my name as a potential candidate to the Sphinx Club of 1989! Now I sit among the brothers and the Jewels honored to be an Alpha man. Honored to be your brother. Thank you very much"

"Are you done brother? Jewel Tandy leans over to Brother Johnson who is seated next to him. He kindly asks his question as he peers over his thin rimmed glasses.

"Oh yes, go right ahead Jewel Brother Tandy!" Denny responds.

"Because I didn't want to cut you off. You sure you're done?" Vertner asks again politely.

Denny laughs. "Oh yes sir. I'm good and done."

"Okay then!" Jewel Vertner Woodson Tandy stands up out of his chair. He is the first brother to stand during the introductions. "Brothers of Alpha! Hear me! I am your Jewel founder, the good brother Vertner W. Tandy!" Everyone laughs as he sticks his chest out as if he is proud of what he just proclaimed. He places his hands into the pockets of his vest and leans back on his heels. This gives his voice more emphasis as he leans into his next statement. "We fought like hell for this organization! You all know that! We know that! Now we see it, not so much in the work that we see in the community. Of course we see it there. Alpha is everywhere! But what I'm talking about is much deeper than that. Much more special. I see it in you!" Jewel Tandy points to me. "I see it in you!" He points to Brother Julian Wilson. "I see it in you!" He points to Brother McCaskill. I see it in each and every one of you here. I saw that thing every time I met an Alpha man. That burning essence that makes him a brother. That thing that makes him fraternity. That spirit that drove us and inspires you."

There is a pause that would normally be awkward. Dead silence. Nobody seems to move. I suppose everyone is surprised that such a passionate response was given in the introductions which have been very light spirited so far. The non-founding brothers are sitting in awe while the six other founders are probably sitting in shock. Vertner has always been the comedian. Someone is waiting for the other shoe to drop.

"Now of course, that same spirit drove many of us to drink!" Vertner laughs loudly at his own joke. The brothers laugh and I notice the founders laughing as if to say "Same ol' Vertner. Same ol' Vertner!" Vertner looks around the room to ensure everyone has enjoyed his jest before he continues. "And speaking of driving to drink, are there libations made available to the Jewels at this feast that has been prepared? If not, one of you young brothers need to drive to get us a drink!" Vertner Tandy takes his seat smiling.

"My brothers, my name is Sean Gayle. I humbly greet you in the true spirit of the fraternity. I'm Beta Chapter, Howard University by way of the Iota Zeta Chapter at the University of Maryland. I'm extremely grateful for my journey and the brotherhood as Alpha has given me something that I never had. I've been accepted and respected as a brother first and foremost and trusted with leadership responsibilities. I was honored to have been elected president of the Kappa Xi Lambda Chapter in New York. We are better known as the Wall Street Alphas. Thank you."

Next is Brother Julian Wilson. "My brothers of Alpha, my name is Julian Wilson. I was initiated into the fraternity in 1980 through the Kappa Phi Lambda Chapter. I'm not certain if many of you are aware of this but I am the grandson of our beloved Jewel founder, Jewel Robert Harold Ogle."

"Really!" Kagi asks and declares at the same time. This causes Brother Wilson to smile.

"Yes. Really." Jewel Ogle answers for Brother Wilson. This is my daughter's son and I'm pleased that he is my fraternity brother as well as my grandson."

With the announcement that Julian Wilson is

actually related to one of the founders, every brother places him in a different category in their mind. How fortunate he must feel to have a blood connection. Every brother of Alpha Phi Alpha has studied these seven men. We have all been taught to memorize their names and at least their occupations after Cornell. We have been told of their contributions to Alpha Chapter and the subsequent chapters to follow. We have read their speeches. We have seen their photos. We know their biographies. We remember their resumes. Brothers can tell you where each is from. We're well versed with the dates and names of things they did. Brothers take pride in how much they can recollect and recite about these seven men. Had it not been for these seven men, many of us who consider ourselves more than brothers would not know each other. Yet none of us have the relationship that Julian Wilson has. None of us are direct descendants. None of us can tell stories of what Robert told his daughter who eventually became his mother. That bond is special. That bond is bigger than black and gold. Its blood.

Julian continues. "I'm pleased to be here. This will be a special conversation and I'm looking forward to hearing the thoughts and expressions that will be shared."

Next is the grandfather. "Good brothers of Alpha Phi Alpha, my name is Bob Ogle. Most of you know me by my full name and Alpha designation, Jewel Robert Harold Ogle. Being here in this meeting in this house is special to me. I moved into this very house, 411 East State Street in the fall of 1905. I was an excited incoming freshman. I was excited to attend Cornell and to continue my education here. Little did I know that something I would be a part of would touch the lives of so many. What we founded became monumental and ground breaking and I am overjoyed to have had that experience with these 6 brothers." Jewel Ogle continues. "I was blessed to meet my lovely wife Helen when I was a sophomore here at Cornell. I met her at an annual event hosted by her family not too far from here. We enjoyed each other and marriage for two years before she passed away. We were blessed to be the parents of two beautiful daughters. I was aided in raising my daughters by Helen's mother and my family and friends. I cannot discount the assistance of my brothers of Alpha Phi Alpha who were there for me at all times. Words simply cannot thank them enough. I'm blessed to know that the brotherhood of Alpha remains in my family as Brother Julian just mentioned, he is my grandson and my fraternity brother. Thank you brothers for your attention."

"Thank you Jewel Ogle." I say solemly. The room is quiet as the next brother begins.

"Brothers my name is Brother Sean L. McCaskill. I crossed into this illustrious organization in the spring of 1990 at the Xi Sigma Chapter at the Indiana University of Pennsylvania. I tell this story often brothers... I was just a kid from the Pittsburgh Hill District Community who was able to defy the odds by earning a football scholarship to attend college. Brothers, right in my freshman year I was having difficulty adjusting to college life. I had no baseline understanding of Greek life at all and in fact brothers, I got into a physical confrontation with several Omegas after a campus party!"

"We all been there bro! Well I can't speak for the Jewels but you know we step up against the Ques when we have to!" Howard jokes as he interrupts Brother McCaskill. Everyone laughs as Howard's comment was made in jest.

"We never backed down from the Omegas either so carry on dear brother, carry on!" The room erupts in laughter as Jewel George Biddle Kelley, who is known to be a feisty fighter, speaks as if he has had confrontations with members of Omega Psi Phi Fraternity. Maybe he has knowing him. I seriously doubt it as he mentions it with a joking tone. Relations in the early days of Black fraternal life were much different than today. An altercation was unheard of although the history books all agree that there were "friendly competitions" between all organizations.

Sean McCaskill is able to continue only after the brothers finish their laughter. Ironically, he is the last to stop laughing. "There was one upperclassmen at IUP who was from Philadelphia that I started to gravitate towards. He basically took me under his wing. He never once told me that he was an Alpha. When I found out that he was a brother, he said these words to me; 'An Alpha man who is doing what the fraternity was founded to do never has to tell the world who he is. The world will know who he is because of the work he does in his community. That's Alpha Phi

Alpha.' After that I was determined to become an Alpha so I could be able to pay it forward. That's my story and of course I'm overjoyed to be here."

"You didn't mention your leadership position in Alpha." Brother Sean's namesake, Sean Gayle states. He reminds Brother McCaskill to mention all of his contributions to the fraternity.

"Oh yes indeed brother! I apologize for not mentioning. I'm the past Eastern Region Vice President and I gave the region of Alpha's birthplace my entire heart. Thank you."

The youngest brother in the house is Brother Kagi Kananga. All eyes focus on him as he introduces himself. "Brothers of Alpha and Jewels, I cannot fully express to you the honor and privilege of being in your presence."

"You sound like you're giving a speech young brother." Howard jokingly states.

Brother Kananga doesn't realize that Howard is joking until the other brothers in the room join in with laughter. It's easy to tell that the laughter is not at the young brother's expense. He smiles and continues. "Yes brother, I guess I'm so used to giving speeches when I'm in the presence of brothers such as yourselves."

"Don't mind Howard." Sean Gayle says. "He can be a..."

"An ass!" Howard finishes Sean's statement.

"I mean, I wasn't gonna say it bruh." Sean replies laughing.

Everyone in the room laughs. Howard laughs louder than anyone as he was clearly joking by finishing Sean's sentence. The brotherly exchange lightens the mood for Brother Kagi who is young in the fraternity. It's so important that young brothers have an opportunity to converse and fellowship with seasoned members of the fraternity. The older brothers will purposely sit in the lobby of the host hotel at conventions and hold conversations that span many hours about their experiences in Alpha. To listen to Alpha wisdom is interesting as the fraternity has changed over the years in many aspects. Developing your own story is equally as important as our oral traditions and the culture of the griot allows us to move stories along. The changes in the fraternity's policies on intake, community enrichment, social media and various other topics create interesting dialogue between brothers of different decades. Brother Kagi expresses that he feels more comfortable simply with his smile. He continues.

"I was initiated into the Alpha Delta Chapter on March 7th, 2015. I am the Western Region Assistant Vice President."

"That is excellent! Great to see young Alpha leadership!" Jewel Callis responds.

"Thank you sir! I'm honored to hear you say that."

"So you're still a college brother." Jewel Murray

asks.

"Yes sir. I attend the University of Southern California and I am in my senior year. I am in the Marshall School of Business and my major is finance and economics with an emphasis on contractual management."

"Wonderful young brother." Jewel Chapman states. Jewel Chapman owned two business while a student at Cornell. He can relate to Brother Kananga who is the only college brother in attendance but more so due to his emphasis on finance.

"Thank you Jewel Chapman! I chose Alpha Phi Alpha Fraternity, Incorporated because of the fraternity's model of uplifting downtrodden humanity and stimulating the ambitions of its members. Alpha has provided me with a vehicle to serve underrepresented communities in the South Central Los Angeles area through financial education and economic development. Furthermore, the ambitions of my fellow brothers motivate me to succeed through hard work and a commitment to an excellent standard unrivaled by any fraternity."

"Yeah bro, you just crossed and you just ran for office!" Brother McCaskill laughs as I'm sure he is thinking back to his days running for office. What Kagi is for the undergraduate brothers on the west, Sean McCaskill served for all of the brothers in the East. Kagi serves as an assistant vice president for the region. Sean served as vice president for the region. Sean more than likely sees a lot of himself in Brother

Kagi. The respect for authority and deference that this young man displays is a strong character trait of every early Alpha. The brothers agree with Brother McCaskill's assessment. "It's good to hear you speak the way you speak Brother Kagi. I've often said, and many brothers can attest that they've heard me say this," Brother McCaskill continues, "that there are two very important days in your life as an Alpha. The two most important days in your Alpha life are the day you cross and the day you fall in love with Alpha. On the day that you cross, you're excited! Whether you were initiated into an undergraduate chapter or on the graduate level. In your mind and in your heart, you've accomplished something great! You've literally aligned yourself with great men. When you think about the acts and deeds of Alpha men over the decades, it almost makes you stop and pause that that man is now your brother. I mean, think about it for a second. Dr. Martin Luther King Jr. is your frat brother. Let that sit for a second and just think on it. All of the great Alpha men that have entered the house of Alpha are your brothers! Paul Robeson is your brother. Jesse Owens is your brother. Duke Ellington is your brother. Donny Hathaway is your brother."

"Preach brother! Preach!" Jewel Vertner encourages Sean and waves his hand toward him like we're in church. The brothers laugh and Sean continues as if he is in church.

"When you think about that crossing date or the first time you put those letters on your chest, it brings chills down your spine! Your crossing date will never change for you. It will always be special and you will celebrate with those that crossed with you, if you weren't a solo, for years to come. Then there's the day you fall in love with Alpha. Whatever that motivation is for you and for each of us, it's different. I can't say what it is for another brother, all I know is what it was for me. It may be socially related. You might fall in love with it while performing in a step show. For me it was the service aspect. Both sides of it. Service to the community that I live in and service to the brotherhood. Man, that got me excited! That's what motivates me. When I see lives being touched by the work of Alpha men, it jump starts me big time. Then when I get to serve the brotherhood through some of the ideas that I have, it's the same feeling. When I can have a team of highly educated and energetic brothers surround me with their ideas and creativity, it motivates me to serve better, do better and be better. So Kagi and all the brothers, tap into that thing that makes us special. Especially in a meeting such as this where we get to sit face to face with our founding fathers and dissect this thing. This is a great opportunity to reconnect and reinvest into this fraternity by learning from our past and pressing into our future."

"Thank you so much brother, I really appreciate what you just said and I will definitely remember that and all that we share today. I definitely have the strong desire to build and share and I too want the betterment of our people through our acts. I love the role that I play for the brothers on the west coast and I hope to build upon an already established great legacy of leadership."

"Oh you will my brother. You absolutely will." Brother Sean McCaskill is a motivational brother in every sense of the adjective. When he speaks to a group of brothers, they hear his heart and connect with his message. There is no mistaking the fire that burns in his heart for Alpha Phi Alpha Fraternity. His mission is to transfer that sentiment to every brother he comes into contact with.

"Brothers, I'm very pleased to be here. My name is William Douglass Lyle. I serve the brothers as the Executive Director and Chief Operating Officer of the fraternity. Before I became the Executive Director and COO, I was the Director of Communications. I did that for nine years. Now in my role as ED, I manage the membership, communications and administration departments; implementing all mandates and resolutions approved by the General Convention. I serve as custodian of all official records of the fraternity including information on each member, secretary to the Board of Directors, and key fundraiser for the fraternity in support of the General President and Board of Directors. I crossed at Xi Chapter seated at Wilberforce University in the spring of 1997. There I was Corresponding Secretary, Vice President, President, and Assistant District Director. It's good to be here and I'm looking forward to a healthy dialogue from both the Jewels and the brothers.

"Brothers, my name is George Biddle Kelley. To

state that I am pleased that the brotherhood has come to this moment in time doesn't substantiate my truest feelings. I am overjoyed with the meeting today. As many of you know, I was the most enthusiastic member of the Society in regard to rendering ourselves a fraternity. I fought tirelessly for the notion. Once approved and welcomed, I became the first president of the chapter. I am honored to have that designation as I am also honored to be a founder of Alpha Phi Alpha. After Cornell, I became the first Black man to be a registered engineer in the state of New York. If there is a major accomplishment in life, I guarantee that an Alpha man did it first!"

"Brothers, it is my honor and esteemed privilege to be here. My name is Darryl Ricardo Matthews Sr. I was initiated on January 27, 1972 at the Delta Rho Chapter. Delta Rho is a metro chapter in Kansas City, Missouri. I'm the past Executive Director for the fraternity and was elected and served as the 32nd General President. I'm happy to be in the number of such extraordinaire gentleman. Brothers of the black and gold, I greet you in the spirit of the fraternity."

"Thank you brothers. Now let us begin. As you're already aware, the purpose of this Jewels Town Hall Meeting is to create dialogue with the founders of the fraternity about the state of the fraternity. We want to discuss brotherhood, community service, mentorship, and whatever other topics come to mind. We also have brothers who are tuned in via Twitter who can submit questions for the founders as well. So without any further adieu, let's begin. I'll throw out the first question to get us started and then brothers can talk as they see fit." Before I begin, I survey the room one final time. I do this to take in the moment. I'm amongst giants at this moment. Leaders in their own personal endeavors and the personification of what these seven founders envisioned in the first place. The bond of brotherhood and the common denominator being Alpha Phi Alpha is astounding to witness. I'm fortunate to be counted among the number and I'm anxious to see where this conversation takes us as a whole. "Question number one. As you look at Alpha Phi Alpha Fraternity over one hundred years after its birth, what similarities and differences do you see with what you had at Alpha Chapter?"

Each of the founders looks at one another to see who will take the first stab at the question.

"I guess I'll answer first." Jewel Robert Harold Ogle is the first to respond. "In Alpha's infancy, I don't believe the brothers knew the jewel, if you will, of what we had accomplished. The early mandate and call to action was the literary society. That idea had its place and definitely has its own merit. The fraternity however, bringing in the aspect of brotherhood took over. We were finding our way in the dark and just trying to figure out what to do next. We had no idea. We had no real blue print to work from. Yes there were our White counterparts who had already been established years prior but that isn't the same. They were not up against the challenges that our students and our people face. To this day the challenges are vastly different. The current day fraternity has the task of addressing the variety of issues that plague our people and Black men in general. Along with that, the duty of policing itself to manage the duties of the organization. I tip my hat to the brothers who have far exceeded my expectations of organization. I don't even know if I answered the question." Everyone chuckles as he smiles.

"I could listen to you all day so please continue." Brother Gayle says.

"The question was to name the similarities and differences from the days of the founding to now. The similarities are definitely the brotherhood. These six gentleman are brothers to me in the truest sense of the word brother. I could not have asked for a finer set of men to attend classes and start an organization with. The differences are the vast number of issues we are dealing with now. I couldn't imagine being at the helm of so great an organization now. Brother Darryl Matthews I salute you for serving as General President in these modern days. I don't think I would want that job."

Brother Matthews smiles and nods. "Thank you sir. I cannot take any of the credit though. The fraternity is filled with brilliant minds and genius ideas. I had a lot of support from both the college and graduate level. I was blessed to lead the brothers into new partnerships and relationships and to continue the great work that you men started. My staff and board held me accountable as I sought to do the work of Alpha and to lead as had been done by so many past

General Presidents."

"I'd like to offer an answer to that question as well." Jewel George Biddle Kelley chimes in. "I feel there are several similarities and differences between Alpha then and Alpha now. First, if you look at some of the things we were up against when the fraternity was founded, our race was up against the wall in a lot of areas. We had laws to change. There were systems that needed to be torn down and redone. There were mentalities that had to be outgrown and in some cases die off. Today the fraternity faces challenges that are markedly different. Racism is now more subtle than it once was. The good old boy network of the past isn't as outwardly vocal with their true feelings. Also, we were concerned with starting the organization. Our concern was making sure the organization existed for years to come on college campuses as far as we could take it. Now you have both college and alumni chapters which normally have different views on things. Existing within one general body with two thoughts can be difficult to navigate but Alphas can stay the course. I also feel that there are striking similarities. There seems to be in a lot of chapters the same general sentiment in chapter meetings that we had in Alpha Chapter. Discussions sound the same. Debates sound the same. No one debates the way Alpha men debate!"

Everyone laughs as we know what he just said is true.

"You got that right good founder!" Brother

McCaskill states. Sean would know as he has been privy to many a debate. He has been a champion on the issues of Alpha at many leadership levels and at the helm of the Alpha Eastern Region during his time as Regional Vice President. "Debates with brothers definitely sharpen my skills! All Alphas are lawyers!"

Jewel Tandy raises his hand and adds. "I'm glad that Alpha is so diverse where we can bring different opinions to the table and be able to still walk away as brothers. No hard feelings and no chips on anyone's shoulders. I don't care if you're a General President, chapter president or president of your college glee club. Every Alpha man is equal in my eyes. No one brother is greater or lesser than another and it's the mutual respect that we have that is the reason behind our greatness."

"I wish it was always like that good brother." Brother Franklin quickly responds. "It's definitely not always like that. I mean, in a perfect Alpha world, yes. But brothers get up in their feelings for sure and a lot of times it comes out verbally. That's why the debates go down the way they do."

"Why don't you elaborate on that Howard?" I want to keep the conversation as fluid as possible so I encourage Howard to continue.

"I'm just saying, I've always been told that everything we ever need is in the house. If you need a doctor, there is an Alpha doctor. If you need a lawyer, there's an Alpha lawyer. So I've seen situations where brothers will bypass and go outside the house and I just wish things were the way the Jewels envisioned it or created it to be. And for Bros to just be real with it."

"That's with any large organization Brother Franklin." Brother Matthews states. Everyone doesn't see things the same way. There's always diversity in thought. It causes one brother to go inside the house to get what he needs or contribute and causes another brother to look elsewhere and pull away. Everyone doesn't think the same way."

"That can both be a good or bad thing." Brother McCaskill adds. I wouldn't want a fraternity of brothers who all thought the same thing. I want to be a part of a progressive brotherhood that's always focused on moving forward with fresh and creative ideas. You cross, you get acclimated, and you get to work! That's how I think it should be."

"I want to answer the question as well. The question about similarities and differences." Jewel Jones says. "I've seen the fraternity take its shape and define what it was to become. To say that Alpha Phi Alpha has accomplished what we set out for it in the beginning is an understatement. We are forever proud of the work that Alpha has provided and the position the fraternity has taken in our community. This to me is very similar to our early days. I remember when the first chapter began to grow and we let brothers diligently work toward our ideals. I remember watching them and being proud that we had developed these men into our brothers. They took the mantle of what we had begun and ran with it."

"Yes indeed. That's very true." Jewel Tandy adds.

There is a slight pause in the discussion which leads me to believe the first question has been exhausted. "The next question for the founders is regarding relations between the other fraternities and sororities. Did any of you know any of the founders of the other organizations? What were the relations between you back then? What do you think of the relations now?" I ask.

"Good question!" Brother Will Lyle has been relatively quiet thus far but speaks up here. As the Executive Director, I know that he has had numerous conversations with leaders from the other Black Greek Letter Organizations. I'm sure he is curious to hear the answer to these questions.

Jewel Callis begins. "I knew Elder Watson Diggs of Kappa Alpha Psi Fraternity. He was a great man. My father pastored the church that he attended in Indiana. I also knew many of the founders of both Alpha Kappa Alpha Sorority and Delta Sigma Theta Sorority. My ex-wife Alice is a Delta. She wrote the Delta hymn. One of the brothers that I knew from Beta Chapter was Brother Numa Adams. He and I were very close friends. Good brother. He married Osceola Macarthy. She is one of the Delta founders. She was a wonderful singer. She performed on Broadway. Wonderful person."

"Wait a minute." Sean Gayle says. "Your ex-wife Alice wrote the Delta Sigma Theta hymn?"

"Yes sir. Their sorority hymn is accredited to my ex-wife." Jewel Callis responds.

"Wow!" Kagi says. "I mean... wow!"

"I bet the brother historians didn't know that huh?" Howard says with a smile. He glances at Brother Harris and Brother Ross.

"I knew it. I know you didn't Kingphish!" Brother Harris responds and causes the brothers to respond in laughter as he uses Howard's nickname.

Jewel Jones brings us back to the question on the floor. "Of course you remember Ethel Lyle and the ladies of Alpha Kappa Alpha Sorority from Howard." Jewel Jones says. "Those ladies were something special! I don't know if I've ever met women with more focus."

Jewel Kelley is next to speak. "Does anyone remember when Omega Psi Phi was founded? How they gave the brotherhood no credit whatsoever?"

"No credit? What do you mean Brother Jewel?" Sean Gayle asked the question that we all were preparing to ask.

"The Omega Psi Phi Fraternity began at Howard and they wrote their history as if to say they were the first to arrive and be founded at a Black college. Now of course, they were right in a sense. They were the first to be founded on a Black college campus. That part is true. They certainly were not the first there however. Our brothers of Beta Chapter, as some of you probably know since it is your chapter of initiation, had been there for a number of years."

"Four years to be exact! The brothers were on Howard's campus for four years before Omega Psi Phi was founded." Jewel Jones adds.

"Our first General Convention was on Howard University's campus in 1908 so what are they talking about?" Kagi adds.

"That is exactly my point Brother." Jewel Jones continues. "Our chapter was already there. The brothers were already on the campus. The dean of men at the time was an honorary member. His name was..."

"Kelly Miller." Jewel Henry Callis states matter of factly.

"Yes, Dean Miller. Dean Kelly Miller was the dean of men and he was made an honorary brother at Beta Chapter. He was on the campus in his position in both 1910 and 1911. To even suggest that Omega Psi Phi was the only fraternity to make the headway as a founding force on the campus is a gross stretch of the truth."

"Damn! That's deep!" Howard responds. "See, I knew them chumps wasn't legit! Wait til I talk to some of my boys that are Ques!" Howard laughs loudly which makes the other brothers in the room laugh as well. "Wait til I see them cat dudes!"

"We have to maintain a mutual respect for the

other organizations. We're all Black men first and foremost. If we choose to go about solving the ills of our community, so be it. We have had to tackle much bigger obstacles than what Greek letters a man sports on his chest and on his varsity jacket. I would think that the fraternity has held to keeping the more important issues at the forefront." Jewel Chapman is already showing himself as the founder with the serious nature. He has been a meticulous mind and a quiet commentator since the onset of Alpha. Always the one to add to the conversation yet the reserved founder who only adds when what is added is necessary. He is a man of few words but his words are always poignant. There's never a question as to what Charles Chapman feels about a topic. He's not ambiguous nor wavering in his opinion. What you see is what you get and what you get is profound.

"As General President, we spend time with the leaders of the other organizations. We attend each other's national conventions and sometimes the regional events. I've always held a good relationship with those leaders who led while I served in office. We definitely have our differences but we celebrate in the things we have in common. We have a lot more in common than we realize. It's those things that give the Black Greek community its strength or whatever strength we're going to have." Words by Brother Matthews. "Although I believe it is important for Alpha to always stand firm in its ability to be the leader amongst leaders, we also need to balance the challenge of not allowing our differences to divide us."

"What about the undergraduates though? I've only been a brother for a short period of time but I see a lot of hate and just... well, hate when it comes to other Greeks my age." The Western Assistant Regional Vice President Brother Kagi asks.

Sean Gayle responds first. "I really wouldn't give it that much attention. Be the best Alpha that you can be and no one will demand any more of you than that. Don't worry about what others are doing. You're gonna see a lot of that hate and immaturity for the first few years. When our young brothers and sisters first enter their organizations, they're excited. They worked long and hard during the semester and paid a lot of money. When they first get their letters and are officially allowed to put them on, it's an amazing feeling. I know every brother in this house right now can attest to that. Even the Jewels. When you first declared Alpha Phi Alpha as an official fraternity on December 4th, a certain feeling came over you. I remember first being allowed to wear my crossing jacket. The letters and the shield were on me for the first time. Prior to that moment, I wouldn't have been allowed to wear those items. I wouldn't even dare sneak and do it. Now though, I'm in a sacred brotherhood and wearing the letters is a right that I earned. So with that, I'm protective. I'm super protective. I fight against an enemy that doesn't even exist. Anyone that I perceive as a threat to my letters or my organization, or my big brothers or my line brothers or chapter, is a threat against me and I don't take that lightly."

"Amen bro!" Howard encourages Sean to continue.

"I'm in several groups on Facebook with a number of young Greeks. I interact with them almost on a daily basis and I see it fresh every year. Some young buck says some off the wall comment and his prophytes will quickly snatch him or her up and bring them back down to Earth. I've been that prophyte many a time for us. I believe I've earned that level of respect from the brothers and some of the other Greeks in NY especially."

"That policing is definitely necessary in this new age of fraternity. We have to police our own and bring em up right. That's so key and so important." Sean McCaskill speaks with passion each time he addresses a topic. He is the kind of Alpha that needs a podium placed in front of him every time he opens his mouth. You can expect Sean the orator to expound on issues that are pertinent to the fraternity. "It's so important that we seasoned brothers lead the newly initiated brothers the right way and keep them on course. That's why this meeting today is so important. We have to get back in touch with our foundation and our roots and you seven men are the reason we're all here. You're the foundation that we all have and what makes us have a common bond. We appreciate you beyond what our words cannot express."

"Thank you good brother!" Jewel Tandy says. "Thank you very much." Vertner nods in Sean's direction.

"I too deal with undergraduates on a consistent basis as my work takes me to campuses all across the country. I lecture and teach on the culture of the Black Greek Organization and what Brother McCaskill shared is so right. There sometimes can be a disconnect with some of the younger members because they lack the internal mentorship that we should all have in place. I try my best to support the undergraduate cause as best I can." Brother Parks indeed has traveled the nation and spoken to members of fraternities and sororities and lent his expertise. As a student of the Black Greek system and a son of the culture, Brother Parks has become a lead expert on matters campus related. His words are not limited to the campus setting but his research has absolutely made him a respected authority on the culture. "I've suggested for many years that somewhat of a one-on-one mentorship model need to be put in place to help foster relations between graduate and undergraduate brothers."

"That's an idea that we spoke of as well as far back as many decades ago." Jewel Jones mentions. "We have long been of the mindset of brotherly mentorship and sponsoring. Is that concept prevalent today within the fraternity?"

Before anyone has a chance to answer, I interject. "Brothers before we embark upon Jewel Brother Jones' question, I want to ask if anyone else wanted to comment on the question about the founders of other organizations. I don't want to hinder the conversation so if it flows to the next question, that's fine. I just want to make sure everyone has had a chance to answer if they wanted to."

"We aren't overly concerned with other founders my brother... move on if ye must! Ye move on!" Jewel Tandy says with a laugh.

Howard Franklin laughs louder than anyone else although we all laugh. "Yes sir! Enough about them! Move on!"

"Move on! Move on! Move on!"

A hysterical chorus of "Move on!" is chanted by the brothers. Even Jewel Chapman smiles as the brothers enjoy a light moment.

Well, let's forge ahead to the next question and we just touched on it a moment ago. What role should mentorship play in Alpha Phi Alpha and what is the best way to implement?"

There is a silence only because more than one founder would like to answer at once and they are being polite as to who responds first.

Jewel Callis responds first. "I remember many conventions in which this very question was asked. The topic has been raised many times. The foundation of Go To High School Go To College is mentorship. We created this organization in part to be a model of mentorship, one to another. In the very early days of the fraternity, we were a literary society. There was nothing in place on campus to help facilitate the matriculation of our community of students through Cornell. We envisioned an atmosphere where Black men could arrive on campus and get the support that they needed. The support that they needed in many times was not provided by the administration. We were to become that support. This is the true essence of the Alpha fraternity. Brotherhood and reaching back to be mentors."

"That's both beautiful and necessary!" Donald chimes in. I love to hear the true purpose of the fraternity. We've all studied it and know it. It's just refreshing to hear it from the mouths of the founders."

"I agree with my brother Henry. That is indeed our mandate from the beginning. It has transitioned over the years." Jewel Ogle says. "That is to be expected. With the change in times, our mandate needs to be adjusted or we become outdated and irrelevant. I believe we have done an excellent job at making that transition. Would you young brothers agree?"

"I would. I definitely think that we have done just that." Denny says. I absolutely agree with our mandate being catered toward what we are accomplishing now. Working through the organization with the Boy Scouts is an example."

"I was going to say the Boy Scout initiative that we have." Wil says. "That's a perfect example. The fraternity makes great strides to create partnerships such as that one to not only foster our initiative of mentorship and community service but to also align ourselves with organizations and partners that will help further our brand and mission. It's a key mission of the leadership of the fraternity to foster relationships that assist us with the mandates that you men set in motion. That is a task that we take serious and that we convey with the rest of the brotherhood."

"Let me say that I am proud of each of you young brothers. The hard work that you have implemented in our vision is refreshing to see." The Jewel of few words, Charles Chapman compliments the brothers.

"I concur." Jewel Murray adds. I've been impressed with the caliber of men that Alpha has attracted and drawn. You brothers and thousands of others are absolutely the best our race has to offer."

"Thank you kind sirs!" Brother McCaskill thanks Jewels Chapman and Murray.

"Is it out of order if I ask a question to the Jewels about something I've wondered about for a long time?" Donald raises his hand like a middle school student.

"No, by all means go right ahead. This is open discussion so it's great if you have a question. After your question, we can go to Twitter and take a question from one of the cyber brothers who submitted."

Donald smiles and thanks me. "Thanks Brother Gourdine. My question can be answered by any of the Jewels." He pauses before he asks his question. "What's the real deal with C.C. Poindexter?"

"Ah hell! This about to get good!" Howard leans forward in his chair and smiles the big Howard Franklin smile that so many brothers are familiar with. He adjusts himself in his chair as if he is preparing to hear something mind blowing and Earth shattering.

Perhaps he is.

Mr. Poindexter has been a mysterious person and rather misunderstood within the annals of the fraternal history. Known as the precursor to the fraternity, he was the graduate assistant who organized these very men into the literary society that was the genesis of Alpha Phi Alpha. It has long been taught that he was never interested in a fraternity. His state of mind was that the Negro student had no place in a collegiate fraternity. The fact that the White students at Cornell and many campuses across the nation had established fraternities and Greek life was irrelevant. It wasn't for the Negro and it could not be a vehicle used to advance the cause. When the determination was made to make the transition from the literary society to the fraternity, Mr. Poindexter submitted a letter of resignation. It is unclear what the letter actually states as history has been told that it was difficult to understand. Nonetheless, he decided to step away and wasn't heard from in terms of Alpha history any longer. His value to the organization is not in the walking away but in the work that he did to organize the group in the first place. Would Alpha Phi Alpha Fraternity be a fraternity with the level of success that it has enjoyed had C.C. Poindexter not done the work of 1905 and 1906? We will never know. What we can glean is how the Jewels feel about Mr. Poindexter from Brother Donald Ross' question.

"Allow me to answer this one." Jewel Callis steps up first to offer an answer.

"No, let's not let you answer first. I'll go first." Jewel Kelley interrupts.

"Excuse me?"

"The brothers may not be able to hear the truth through your obvious p.p."

"My what?"

"Your Poindexter propaganda!"

Jewel Tandy laughs and looks over his round rimmed glasses as if to say "Uh oh..."

"I beg your pardon brother but if anyone can speak on Brother C.C., it's me. I knew him more than any of you and whether you wish to acknowledge his contributions to our organization or not, that doesn't negate the contribution." Jewel Callis returns. Jewel Callis has had his demeanor change in an instant. Clearly this is a topic of much debate between the founders. The slightest mention of the name C.C. Poindexter has caused two Jewel founders to begin to debate with one another as to who should speak first.

"First of all, he is not a brother. He is not and has never been duly initiated into the Alpha Phi Alpha Fraternity. So you do realize it is disrespectful to refer to him as brother." It seems as if Jewel Kelley may have been one of the strongest proponents for the fraternity vs the literary society, making him antagonistic to Mr. Poindexter. History teaches that debates were long and heated as the two concepts went back and forth between the Cornell students and Professor Poindexter.

"Okay brothers wait, we need not do this in front of the young brothers." Jewel Ogle tries to settle the debate before it really ensues.

"We're all brothers in the room and I dare not believe that every brother in here has not been witness and privy to a... healthy disagreement in a chapter meeting." Jewel Kelley chooses his words wisely as he makes his statement. He knows that every brother has seen a chapter disagreement with the exception of maybe Brother Kagi Kananga. Brother Kagi is so new to the fraternity that he may not have seen many of the chapter interactions. Other than that, we should all be too familiar with fraternal disagreements, arguments, and... heated disagreements.

"How about I'll answer first. I'm objective and I really don't care if you brothers like my opinion or not. You guys can follow me and fight about who will go second." Jewel Chapman quiets the entire room and ends the debate between Callis and Kelley. He ends the debate for now at least. They can resume the debate for position number two at his conclusion. "C.C. Poindexter had good intentions. He had the right idea but was more than likely a little untimely. What he possessed in passion, he lacked in vision. What he had in organizational skills, he didn't have in foresight. What he clearly had in leadership skills, he didn't have at all in brotherhood. Did we need him in those early days? Yes. I would say absolutely. Could we exist without him as a fraternity? Clearly. If we couldn't, would we be gathered today?"

"I know a lot of brothers today that probably don't need to be in the house. If C.C. Poindexter had made his own frat, they would probably be better suited for that. Poindexter Phi Poindexter or something!" Howard blurts out. Everyone laughs especially Howard who laughs louder than everyone else.

"Poindexter never saw the big picture. I remember days when I thought about brothers like the ones gathered in this room. I didn't know what caliber of men we would attract but I felt that we should set a standard for what we were and likeminded individuals would follow. Now when I meet General President Darryl Matthews and the author Gregory Parks. Speaking with Brother Harris before this meeting officially started was an amazing few minutes for me."

"I'm humbled Jewel Kelley." Brother Robert Harris interrupts Jewel Kelley. "I'm truly humbled."

"I'm honored that you are a member of this great fraternity and the national historian. Alpha Phi Alpha Fraternity is in good hands. You gentlemen are the reason we chose to start this organization. Mr. Poindexter didn't see that. He didn't have the foresight."

Jewel Callis has allowed Jewel Kelley to finish before he counters. "I don't agree with my brother's assessment. George and C.C. were always at odds and both are entitled to their opinion. I have great respect for both men. I can't say for certain we would be assembled in this very estate if it had not been for the early efforts of C.C. Poindexter. Had he been a man of no vision, would we have had a literary society? Had we not formed a literary society, would I know any of you brother founders? Would any of you know me? Would we have a fraternity if that had never happened? Would we still revere December 4th and embrace that date in fraternal awe?"

"No. Without Poindexter, our date would have been October 4th!" Vertner jokes that Alpha Phi Alpha would have been founded a lot earlier if it wasn't for the delays attributed to Poindexter's vote. The room erupts in laughter, even Jewel Chapman. The laughter is a great way to break a little of the tension that the Poindexter question has caused. As expected, the topic of C.C. Poindexter is a sensitive topic from the early days to today.

"I remember when the question was being raised as to who the actual seven Jewels were going to be. Based on contributions from the early years, the correct designation has been made. We are the seven who had the most to contribute to Alpha Phi Alpha and should be standing as the forefathers. Mr. Poindexter's name doesn't belong in that discussion as he chose to walk away at a time when we were forming." Jewel Jones has always been proud that he was given the honor of being a Jewel in 1952. He would consider it the highest level of disrespect if he had not gotten the designation in favor of C.C. Poindexter.

"All I know is, I met some Poindexter bros in my

day. That's all I'm gonna say on that." Howard says with a smile. Although he smiles, the brothers know that he is serious.

Every brother knows that they've met a brother or two who has remained inactive for reasons most of us consider excuses. Each of us can attest to knowing brothers who are no longer involved that swore when they were initiated that their decision to become and Alpha was a lifelong commitment of service. For a variety of reasons that could be considered legitimate or excuses, many have fallen by the wayside. Perhaps some have chosen to silently walk away when the experience of fraternity wasn't what they thought it was. Do these brothers embody what C.C. Poindexter must have felt when his friends decided to take the organization in a different direction than what he originally intended?

C.C. Poindexter became a representation of things to come just as it can be said Jewel Jones represented all brothers who would lead a national civic organization or Jewel Tandy represented all brothers who became architects. Poindexter may have been credited falsely as cowardly walking away when in actuality, many of the early decisions that led to the formation of the fraternity are the direct result of his leadership. The proper use of parliamentary procedure, the meeting documentation and archival of records, the meticulous treasury, and other basic meeting criteria were somewhat foreign to young Cornell students. It was Poindexter who added structure and foundation to the Alpha Phi Alpha Society. His involvement and participation has always been at the heart of debate as to how he should be remembered and revered if at all.

"I wish to add to the discussion." Jewel Murray leans forward and raises his hand but begins speaking before he is acknowledged to speak. "I've never been of the mindset that Professor Poindexter should be even named with the rest of us. I would have never been comfortable with that. The point is that we would still be a society of Cornell students who have gathered reading materials had it been left to him. No other campuses. Nothing more. No insight. Nothing in comparison to what we have accomplished. Over one hundred years and look at what our fraternity... and I emphasize the word fraternity has done! The long list of notable brothers is unmatched. The fact that Alpha Phi Alpha Fraternity stands at the forefront of other organizations is quite a distinction. The first and the best to do it. Other organizations can thank us for our contribution to them. How can we hang that on the shoulders of a man who one day served as our president and leader and the next day walked away?" This is the most that Jewel Murray has shared on any topic. This topic has awakened the room and caused everyone to sit up in their seat and pay close attention. Of course sitting with the Jewel founders is exciting enough. No one has dozed off or daydreamed. We linger on every word of these talented men. Everything they say has gone in one of our ears and not come out the other.

"I'm certainly glad I asked this question!" Donald says.

"Me too!" Sean McCaskill adds.

"Bruh!" Sean Gayle responds as well. Sean's one word response says so much. The term can be used to cosign the sentiments of another brother. It can be used to show disdain. It can be used in admiration. There are many uses in this all-encompassing word. In this context, Sean fully agrees with his namesake Sean McCaskill and speaks for many of us with "Bruh!"

"Wait a minute brother!" Jewel Callis's voice is raised. "I'm not going to allow you to taint the view of these brothers outside of the proper context. Allow them to know the whole story and then make up for themselves the proper narrative."

"The whole story? What whole story is there when we were there! We are the whole story!" Jewel Murray spiritedly responds back.

"We are the whole biased story. Each of us has a bias for or against this topic but at least we have the entire context. These brothers do not." Jewel Callis responds. "It's not fair to tell a one-sided tale as if that is the totality of the truth when indeed it isn't."

"Speak on it Jewel Callis! Speak on it!" Howard encourages Jewel Callis to say what he is trying to say.

"Yes Henry. Say what you're trying to say. There is no holding back among the brothers. We've always been open to discuss."

Jewel Callis pauses as if he wishes to consider whether he should continue down the road that this conversation has placed him on. What feels like a long pause really is nothing more than a few seconds yet everyone can tell that he chooses his words carefully. "Everything that these brothers know of C.C. Poindexter and what we... or they I should say... feel about him is based on what they've read in the various editions of the history book written by Charles. Charles wrote the history book in 1929 but in the March 1922 issue of the Sphinx, you all should remember that it was a directory issue. In that issue, we listed living and deceased members. The issue listed four brothers who were alumnus of Alpha Chapter who are now in the Omega Chapter for deceased brothers. C.C. Poindexter is one of those four brothers."

"What? Really?" Brother Kagi surprisingly says. His eyes are now wide and his mouth is a little ajar. He didn't close it after the word really left his lips.

"So Poindexter is listed in the issue as a brother?" Wil asks.

Jewel Callis responds. "Yes. Seven years after the issue was published in The Sphinx, the first edition of The History of Alpha Phi Alpha: A Development in Negro College Life is published by Brother General President Charles Wesley. It then states what it states, that C.C. was never a brother and the..." Jewel Callis searches for the proper word to convey his thought. "...impression is given that there was disdain between us and him. In him walking away, he did so with his head bowed and defeated. We that were there know that C.C. was not a defeated man nor was he a push over. We all know that. Whether we agreed with his premise or not, none of us nor he were easily swayed."

"You certainly make your point there!" Jewel Tandy says with a laugh. "Preach on preacher man."

"Okay but Jewel Callis, or whoever chooses to answer, why would the history book give one impression and The Sphinx indicate that something else may be the case?" Denny asks.

Jewel Callis responds. "Remember brothers that C.C. went on from Cornell University and began teaching at Fisk University. In the year 1909, he had a student who didn't do too well in his course. Matter fact, that student told me that Professor Poindexter's class proved to be the worst grade that he got that entire semester. This student always maintained the highest scholastic standards and was always hard on himself for any less. He became an Alpha man and a scholar. He absolutely lines up with the ideals of the fraternity in that he saw his work as the most important and vital piece to his collegiate existence. Receiving that score of a 78... I believe it was in that course, really took a toll on him."

"I'm sorry but I don't follow. With all due respect good brother, what does that have to do with Mr. Poindexter and the history book?" Denny follows his question with this follow up.

"That student was Charles Wesley. The author of the history book."

"Damn!" Brother Howard Franklin makes a loud proclamation to the surprise of some in the room. Those that are surprised at his outburst are probably not as familiar with his character. This is Howard and what you see is what you get with him. Passion and enthusiasm are two adjectives that readily describe him. As he is surprised, so is the responses he provides. "See, this is why I'm here! Damn! Sitting at the footsteps of the Jewels and hearing this is no joke! Yes sir! So let me get this straight..."

"Howard calm down. You don't have to be so loud." Wil speaks to Howard with a smile but we all know that he is serious. This meeting needs to maintain order and decorum. With so many personalities and age ranges in the room, the likelihood of things going array is a strong possibility. That hinders the discussion and that is definitely a concern of leadership. Brother Wil Lyle hasn't shared much as of yet. He is a silent leaders in many aspects but a very astute brother with the weight of the fraternity on his shoulders at all times. He is a warm brother that will always spend minutes discussing with brothers over a friendly brotherhood smoke. He takes the business seriously and enjoys the fraternalism as well.

"Calm down? I'm just sayin' bruh. I can't ask the Jewel my question?" Howard responds directly to Wil.

Wil nods to Howard as if to suggest that he can continue. Not that Howard needed permission. Not that Howard would've stopped if he were not allowed to continue.

"So why though? That's a hell of an allegation."

"My attempt is not to create any theories of conspiracy or to tarnish any good brother. Neither of those brothers are present to defend their good name and I'm not here to rehash old ideas or open wounds. What I am suggesting is that we not paint a glorified picture for brothers to sway them either way." Jewel Callis is a politician when it comes to making a point. He never entered the political arena but if he had, I believe he would have been successful. "With that being said however..." In true political fashion, Callis smiles as he indicates he is about to trump everything he just said. "Seven years separated the event of The Sphinx directory and the publishing and release of our history book. One has Mr. Poindexter as an alum of Alpha Chapter and in the Omega Chapter as a deceased brother and one has him almost as an outcast. The history book was penned by respected General President and historian Charles Wesley who we all know and love yet he clearly had bias. He may have had his own personal agenda and the only founders he reached out to in order to complete the work were the two that lived in Washington near him. You were one of them my brother." Jewel Callis looks at Jewel Nathaniel Murray.

Jewel Murray is originally from Washington, DC and lived there during the 1920's. When Charles H. Wesley began his work on developing the Alpha history book, Murray was one of only two founders that lived in Washington. Wesley was able to speak directly with the two founders who were in close proximity to him. It had been rumored that Murray and Poindexter were at odds because Poindexter taught agriculture on the collegiate level and Murray taught it on the high school level. Poindexter often carried an air of egotistical confidence about him which gave people the impression that he thought he was better than the others. There may have been friendly competition between Poindexter and Jewel Murray which spilled into a disdain. Jewel Murray may have offered a rather biased opinion to Brother Wesley as he was preparing to document the history. The only documented proof of this is the manner in which Murray spoke of Poindexter before and after the founding date. Jewel Murray never hid his feelings toward Mr. Poindexter and the belief is that he wasn't too upset when Poindexter decided to resign with regret.

I want to give Jewel Murray or any other Jewel for that matter a chance to respond. The pause after Jewel Callis speaks is much louder than the silence itself. It's loud like a concert yet silent like a moment of silence. As I prepare to break the silence, someone breaks it for me.

"I knew this meeting would be interesting to say the least. I however, wasn't expecting what has happened so far and I'm very happy to be a part of this. Speaking with the founders on these topics is epic and the opportunity should not be taken lightly. Instead, rather reverently as what is being shared is timeless as well as important. These responses and this dialogue is relevant to Alpha's history and timely for Alpha's presence in society today. To know so well from where we have come gives us indication that so much more can and should be done. We are talented and gifted. Most of all, we are blessed by God to accomplish a mission to transcend all by serving all of mankind. God enables us by giving us the power to do so and we decide through the spirit of brotherhood to do it." Julian speaks eloquently yet direct. His point is well made and taken.

"Brothers, let's move on to another question." I state. I'm happy to move on yet I celebrated that spirited debate just now. That truly gives me some insight as to the inner workings of the Jewels and how their meetings must have been. The mutual respect is there but no one holds their tongue. There should be no allusion that these gentlemen were under a peace treaty and conducted themselves in meetings like they were soft spoken monks. On the contrary, each founder is not afraid to speak and give his opinion, even if his opinion isolates him. These seven men are unapologetic and unafraid. Nothing I ask or bring up will shake them... and that's a good thing.

"Brothers, we have brothers from all over the country who are excited about the Alpha Town Hall Meeting. Through modern technology, they are able to send in questions or comments for the Jewels. Right now, I want to go to Twitter and get our first cyber question. It comes from..." I look at my phone. "Our first question comes from @onesmoovealpha.

@onesmoovealpha wants to know if any of the Jewels are impressed by any particular Alpha brother they have met in their travels.

"I'll answer that." Jewel Kelley speaks first. "I have to say that I've met so many brothers who have impressed me. Far more accomplished than I. If I had to name someone who impressed me the most, I'd have to say it is..."

"C.C. Poindexter?" Gregory blurts out Mr. Poindexter's name which causes all Alpha brothers, both Jewel founders and brothers in the room to erupt in laughter. Especially Jewel Tandy who is laughing louder than anyone else.

"Brother Parks, you're alright with me! You beat me to it!" Jewel Tandy says between hearty laughs.

Jewel Kelley regains control of the conversation after another full minute of laughter. "I was most impressed with Brother Dr. Martin Luther King Jr. He spoke at the 50th anniversary convention. Brother King was an awesome orator. That was a great speech."

"Yes it was!" Jewel Callis adds. "He captivated the entire room!"

Jewel Kelley continues. "Meeting a person like Dr. King was an exhilarating experience. He was a giant among mere men. A real brother's brother and proud to be an Alpha man. Yet when he took the platform, his words came to life and energized an entire generation. What a great brother."

"Wow!" Denny says.

"There were so many Alphas of influence during the Civil Rights era. Dr. King stood at the forefront," Donald says, "and he was assisted by Alpha men like Brother Wyatt T. Walker, Brother Marion Barry and Brother Joseph Lowery."

"There goes an Alpha man!" Sean McCaskill proclaims.

"Indeed!" Julian adds.

"I'd like to answer the question." Jewel Ogle responds.

"Sure, go right ahead." I say.

"Thank you. I remember meeting Brother Belford Lawson. Now there was a dynamic brother!" Jewel Ogle states definitively.

"The Belford V. Lawson Oratorical Contest!" Denny states proudly. Denny is a public speaker and does motivational speaking engagements often. He's been invited to speak at many of the Alpha regional and national conventions. With a message of mentorship and brotherhood, Denny is a sought after speaker. The Jewels would be proud if they ever had the opportunity to hear Denny speak. If there is ever a General President that Denny would admire its Brother Belford V. Lawson Jr for the oratorical contest held at Alpha conventions.

"Yes, I've heard the name because of the oratorical

contest at nationals and through my study of the history of the fraternity when I was in my journey to become a brother." Kagi adds. Being a new brother in the fraternity, the history of the organization is still very fresh in his mind. Every brother need to be as well versed as they can be on the history of the fraternity. Knowing your history prevents you from repeating bad behaviors and opens the mindset to creating good ones. It also creates a sense of pride when you remember the awesome accomplishments of the brothers.

"Yes sir!" Jewel Ogle continues. "Brother Lawson who also served as General Present was a dynamic and gifted brother! I think most brothers that know of him know him as either the GP or because of the speaking contest but how many of you knew that Brother Lawson is the first Black man to win a case before the Supreme Court?"

"What! I didn't know that!" Sean Gayle states.

"I didn't know that either." Howard says. "I bet more bros don't know that."

"I knew it." Donald proudly says with a smile.

"I knew it too." adds Brother Harris.

"Well of course you guys knew it! Y'all supposed to know it! Y'all the history buffs!" Howard says laughing.

Jewel Ogle smiles as he continues. "Belford was a great man. He was the first Black man to be president of the Y."

"The what?" I ask.

"The YMCA."

"Belford Lawson was president of the YMCA?" I ask surprised.

"Yes. I told you he was a dynamic man and a true asset to Alpha Phi Alpha Fraternity." Jewel Ogle is speaking as proud of Brother Belford Lawson as if he was speaking about his own son. He has good reason to brag. Belford Lawson represents the best of the best of what Alpha has to offer. When studying the legacy of the fraternity, an exemplary example of a true Alpha man is Brother General President Lawson. He continues. "Many brothers may not know that he was very much involved in the helping of brothers in the legal arena. He was instrumental in getting the authorization for Brother Thurgood Marshall to file the case of Murray vs. Maryland. The University of Maryland School of Law would be required to allow segregation in its colleges if Brother Thurgood won that case. Of course, he won so segregation became a requisite. The gentleman we fought for, Donald Murray, was admitted to the school as the first African American to attend the college."

"Was Mr. Murray a brother of Alpha?" Jewel Ogle's grandson Julian asks.

"No he wasn't. That was one of the beauties of helping with this case. We work for all mankind, not just brothers. Brother Thurgood was passionate in his presentation and direct in his delivery. It was a great day for the race when Brother Belford and Brother Thurgood put their heads together for the betterment of the race."

"Wow, that's awesome. A good piece of history to know." Denny says.

"Yes it is. This is what it's all about! The better making of men!" Sean McCaskill adds.

"If I may, I would like to mention the brother who you just mentioned, Brother Thurgood Marshall." Jewel Chapman states. "I'm very much impressed with him."

"Before you proceed George, I just have one more thing I'd like to add if that suits you kind sir." Jewel Ogle interrupts to add one final point.

"Sure. Go right ahead."

"I'd like to add that I'm impressed with my grandson, Brother Julian Wilson. I'm impressed with his spirit and decorum. He is a gifted and talented man and I appreciate him being a member of both my family and my fraternity."

"It is both an honor and a privilege to be related to a Jewel founder of Alpha Phi Alpha Fraternity. Thank you for your words. They mean a lot to me... my brother and my grandfather."

What a moment! Speechless doesn't describe it. The meeting continues.

Jewel Chapman makes the next point. "I'm very

impressed with Brother Thurgood Marshall. What a powerful brother!"

"Absolutely! Alpha's finest!" Sean Gayle states.

"To eloquently argue the cases that he argued was brilliant of itself. A genius mind! To garner the respect to be the first Black person selected to the Supreme Court is an incredible accomplishment indeed."

Jewel Tandy chimes in. "Like Brother Charles mentioned, the accomplishment is incredible. See, in our era, there are a lot of first Blacks to do certain things. The first Black person on the Supreme Court. The first Black person to win a case in front of the Supreme Court. The first Black to do this and the first Black to do that. When Alpha stands at the forefront of those conversations, it makes us all proud."

The beauty of Jewel Vertner Woodson Tandy is that he can hold an intelligent conversation about life, the Black community or architecture. In the next instance, he can run off a series of jokes that will have you holding yourself in laughter. He can tell you that we need to fight until hell freezes over and then tell you that we then need to fight on the ice! The dichotomy of Vertner.

"Thurgood Marshall is absolutely a hero of mine." says Darryl Matthews. "He was of a pioneer mind and I love that about him."

"Here! Here!" adds Denny. That's a well-respected brother right there. Most brothers brag on Dr. King first and Brother Thurgood second."

"I've had conversations with some of my friends who are members of other fraternities. We brag on our famous members and compare all the time. There have been times where I will be prepared to list the famous brothers of Alpha and they will say that I cannot state Dr. King nor Thurgood Marshall because the contest wouldn't be fair." The brothers laugh as I make the following statement. "But aren't they Alphas? Why you mad?"

Everyone in the room laughs. My statement holds truth. No fraternity can stick out its collective chest and brag on its members the way Alpha Phi Alpha can. Brothers will automatically state Dr. Martin Luther King Jr. first. That's expected. That's a given. Dr. King is the only American with a national holiday. Once George Washington's and Abraham Lincoln's days were combined to create President's Day, that left only Dr. Martin Luther King Jr.'s day as the sole holiday. When the MLK Memorial was built in Washington, DC, it was an unmatched accomplishment. The fraternity had the task of raising the funds, securing the designer and builder, getting the adoption from the Parks Department and having it signed off by a United States President. At the official groundbreaking event, there were three United States Presidents in attendance; George H. Bush, George W. Bush and Bill Clinton. The King family attended the event. Rev. Jesse Jackson was there. Rev. Al Sharpton was there. Alpha man Andrew Young was there. Oprah Winfrey walked in with Patti LaBelle. All of the living General

Presidents of Alpha Phi Alpha were there. The CEO of Delta Airlines was there. The Commissioner of the National Basketball Association was there. I attended the groundbreaking and as I walked in, I noticed that there was a gate in the front where people were being turned away. Only certain people could get past the gate to witness the event up close. I approached the gate and was stopped by security. I was then told that the only credentials allowed past the gate were the media (magazine, television and radio) and brothers of Alpha Phi Alpha Fraternity. I was allowed past the gate once I showed my membership card. That was a proud moment for me. The event was a proud moment for our fraternity. The holiday is a proud day for our nation. The monument is a proud moment for the world. Once brothers exhaust Brother Dr. Martin Luther King Jr. and Brother Thurgood Marshall, you may hear names such as Brother Adam Clayton Powell Jr., Brother Jesse Owens, Brother W.E.B. DuBois, Brother Andrew Young, Brother Cornel West, Brother John H. Johnson, Brother Duke Ellington, Brother Donny Hathaway, Brother David Dinkins, Brother Lionel Richie, Brother Omari Hardwick, and of course Brother Mal Goode.

"I'd like to answer the question from the brother if I may. I'd have to say that I am most impressed with Brother Dick Gregory." Jewel Murray says.

"Oh yeah! Man talk about a powerful brother!" Sean McCaskill responds. "Political activist! Community activist! Hero! I mean I remember him fasting for the cause! I thought he was gonna die but he's still here raising awareness! Man I love that bro!"

"But the interesting thing about Brother Gregory is that he didn't start out as a political activist or a conspiracy theorist. Not at all. He started as a comedian."

"Oh yeah, I knew that good Jewel brother." Sean says smiling.

"Right. Most people know that Brother Gregory started in comedy but listen to some of the things that make him special. Like it was mentioned earlier, I too love to announce when Alpha men are the first at something. The first Black man to do this was an Alpha man! I love that. Well, when Brother Dick first started doing stand-up comedy, he was offered an opportunity to perform his routine on The Tonight Show. A gentleman named Jack Paar was the host back in those days. You young brothers don't remember that particular host I'm sure. Well the show back then was well known to help aspiring entertainers get their start in the entertainment business. It would be like launching your career to the next level. At that time however, Black comedians could perform on the show but were never asked to sit on the couch afterward to talk to the host. That was for White comedians only. When Brother Gregory was asked to perform on the show, he declined the invitation. He declined several times, one after the other. Finally, the show host called him personally to find out why he would refuse such a grand opportunity. Brother Gregory told Jack that he would not perform on the show unless he could also sit on the famous couch and talk to him afterward. Jack went back to the producers of the show and they agreed to let Brother Gregory perform. Brother Gregory was the first Black person to sit on the couch for an interview and that spurred conversations all across America!"

"See I never knew that! That's fascinating!" Denny states.

"I didn't know that either." I state. I had always thought of Brother Dick Gregory as a conspiracy theorist. He's had some great points in his lectures so I wouldn't write him off but a theorist nonetheless. However I never knew this bit of historical information regarding him. There goes an Alpha man!

"Jewel brothers, please continue! Who else has impressed you or motivated you in Alpha Phi Alpha?" Donald asks.

"I will go next." Jewel Callis has been observing his fellow Jewels speak highly of notable brothers of Alpha Phi Alpha. It is noticeable how this particular part of the conversation has warmed his heart as he has smiled and seemingly stared away into space as brothers speak. It's as if he is remembering his times with these notable brothers.

"I would like to mention a good brother who lived up to the ideals of Alpha on a consistent basis. Brother Stuart Scott."

"Oh hell yeah!" Howard says loudly. "Brother Scott

was the man on Sportscenter! I loved him! Always reppin' the frat big time!"

"Say that! Yeah he was!" Denny cosigns what Howard says. "I loved ESPN specifically because of Brother Scott!"

Jewel Callis continues. "Now here is a brother that remained who God created him to be in the face of people trying to change him. The media had never seen a broadcaster that spoke in his own personal style the way Brother Scott would. He brought himself to his profession and did it with style, class and conviction the way an Alpha man is supposed to! Makes us very proud to see a brother walking in his light the way God intended! He received so much hate mail yet refused to be anyone else than who he was created and destined to be. That's what we created! Men unafraid to stand against opposing odds."

"There was a time when a few professional athletes were critical of Stuart when he used some of his hip hop and catch phrases. Before it became popular, he was widely criticized. Once he popularized it and it went mainstream because of Sportscenter, everyone all of a sudden was on board with him." Wil brings a good point. Stuart Scott brought a generation of young people who connected to him through hip hop to ESPN. He also opened the door for many young Black journalists to be able to be themselves and not to be conformed into what the media industry wanted them to be. It isn't uncommon now to hear a sports analyst quote lyrics from popular hip hop songs as they broadcast a game. Stuart Scott is the genesis of that. As the Jewels have said, the first to do it is an Alpha. There goes an Alpha man!

When Stuart was diagnosed with a debilitating disease, he fought it head on. He displayed courage that many never are able to display or witness. His now famous quote, 'When you die, it does not mean that you lose to cancer. You beat cancer by how you live, why you live, and the manner in which you live.' will live on in the hearts of many.

Jewel Callis continues. "What most impressed me about Brother Scott is how he left a legacy which we all should be striving to do. His daughters created the campaign Raised by an Alpha Man and to see the thousands of responsible fathers take to that mantle was heartwarming for the founders. We are so proud to watch the brothers come from the teenage years of undergraduate membership to the leadership positions in the fraternity. What makes us even more proud is to watch the young brothers take their right place in their homes, with their families and in their communities. It is a strong and beautiful thing and Brother Scott transferred very well."

"That's an awesome testimony to a powerful brother! God bless his children and family." Jewel Jones adds. He decides to continue the topic. "If I may, I'd like to offer a brother who I'm so impressed with. Brother Marc Morial of the National Urban League."

"Of course you'd say him! Isn't the brother your predecessor?" Jewel Tandy says with a smile.

"And that is exactly why he is my favorite!" Jewel Jones answers back.

There is a slight chuckle among the brothers as Jewel Eugene Kinckle Jones continues. "It's not just the Urban League. Granted, I am the architect of the League and he is at the helm. That is assuring indeed! Brothers of Alpha have always been in key leadership positions in the National Urban League, starting with the CEO. I admire that greatly and it makes me proud to not only be a brother but to be a founder of that organization as well. That however is not why I nominated the brother as an Alpha who I am impressed with. As impressive of an accomplishment as that is. I more am impressed by the relationship he and his father shared."

"Really? Why is that Brother Jewel Jones?" Kagi asks.

Donald answers before Jewel Jones does. "Brother Marc Morial's father is Brother Ernest Dutch Morial. He was the 23rd General President of Alpha and the Mayor New Orleans. His son Marc is also a brother and was also the Mayor of New Orleans."

"That's exactly right Brother Ross! Quite the historian you are! I may have to reconsider my vote and cast it to you as the Alpha who most impresses me!" Jewel Jones is joking as made clear by his gesture and tone. Donald smiles a large smile and contests the Jewel's remarks.

"Oh no, you are far too kind my Jewel! Please leave

that vote with Brother Morial where it belongs! Leave it right there!"

Everyone laughs.

"You can put that vote on me if you want! Hell, if Bro Donald don't want it, I do!" Howard finds it easy to find humor in many things. He once again has the brothers laughing loudly. I can't say I don't agree with him.

"Man you a fool bro!" Gregory says to him.

"Brother you remind me of a young Vertner." says Jewel Callis.

"With all due respect Jewel Callis I think I'm more like Jewel George Biddle Kelley! I heard he would get up in your face, not hold his tongue and let you know what's on his mind at any given moment. He might even throw a chair in a meeting!"

Jewel Kelley smiles. The brothers are still laughing.

"Brother, in that case, you remind me of a young George!" Jewel Callis responds.

The room erupts in laughter. After the laughter subsides, Jewel Jones continues. "I have a true affinity for the father son relationship of the brothers of Alpha. I am honored to be the only Jewel that was able to induct both my father and son into Alpha Phi Alpha. That is an honor that I cherish with all my heart. To now witness so many brothers follow in the footsteps of their fathers, grandfathers, uncles, mentors, coaches, principles, and other role models is heartwarming and encouraging."

Jewel Jones is extremely passionate when he discusses the lineage of the Jones family. It is apparent to the brothers in attendance that he loves his father, son and brothers of Alpha.

"Brother Dutch Morial had a heart for people. Let me tell you young brothers what this brother means to the hearts and minds of so many and what he means to Alpha Phi Alpha. First of all, I hope you brothers are recognizing a theme in all that your founders are saying. We are the first is not just an expression for brothers of Alpha. It is what we live by. So many brothers that we have mentioned are the first in their particular field of endeavor. That is not an accident my brothers, that is who we attract. That is what we set out to attract as founders. Dutch Morial is the first Black person to graduate and receive a law degree from the law school at LSU."

"Wow! I didn't know that!" Denny says.

"I didn't know that either!" I proclaim.

"Yes sir he was. But wait, there's a lot more. He became the first Black member of the Louisiana State Legislature since Reconstruction. Next he became the first Black Juvenile Court judge in Louisiana. Then he became the first Black American elected to the Louisiana Fourth Circuit Court of Appeal."

"My brother! Wow!" Kagi responds.

"I knew the family legacy was special," says Sean Gayle, "but I have to admit that I didn't know Dutch Morial was the first African American man to accomplish so many things."

"See this is remarkable and this is indeed what Alpha is about. You can't tell me that every brother in this room doesn't have goosebumps on their arm and the hair standing straight up on the back of their neck from hearing all this! Whether you knew the particular facts or not, that is almost not the point. Did you hear what our Jewel just told us? Have y'all heard what these men have been pouring into us for the last hour? Alpha Phi Alpha is all about leaders and leadership and that's not something we just preach now! These Jewels are dropping jewels, no pun intended! They here letting us know that we have to continue to develop leaders and strive for excellence in all that we do! This is a must for all Alpha men everywhere!"

When Brother Sean McCaskill just mentioned 'no pun intended', I believe in normal circumstances there would be a laugh. In this instance, the tone is so serious and his posture demands such attention that laughter is not the flavor of the moment. This is Alpha Phi Alpha and we are in the midst of hearing about greatness from greatness! What a benefit and a blessing to be counted among the brothers when you hear of such accomplishments!

Jewel Jones continues. "So a list of firsts are customary for the Morial brothers. Brother Ernest...

or Dutch as he was called then became the first Black mayor of New Orleans. That is a major accomplishment! Listen brothers! He was so beloved by the people of not only New Orleans but Louisiana in general that the Convention Center was renamed the Ernest Dutch Morial Convention Center! If you ever travel down to New Orleans, know that the Convention Center is named after an Alpha man! Know that the Convention Center is named after a General President!"

"This fraternity is incredible! One of the best decisions I've ever made!" Kagi states proudly.

"Never let that fire be extinguished young brother! The same passion you feel about Alpha Phi Alpha today need to be the same passion you feel when you reach your 50th anniversary as a brother! Let that be a mandate for you to live by!" Jewel Murray offers sound advice to Brother Kananga. Kagi smiles and receives it well.

"I need to also bring to the brother's attention that Brother General President has another first under his belt! Brother Dutch was the first Black person inducted into the Louisiana Political Museum and Hall of Fame! Truly there goes an Alpha man! First! Leader! Alpha! Now moving on to his son Marc," Jewel Jones continues, "who became a brother and in his father's footsteps, became the mayor of New Orleans. Brother Marc served two terms as mayor of New Orleans and his next accomplishment was to become President and CEO of my think tank, the National Urban League."

The National Urban League was formed generally

during the time that Alpha Phi Alpha was founded and becoming established. In 1918, Jewel Eugene Kinckle Jones took over the leadership of the organization. The organization expanded significantly under his leadership and held fast to its mission; to enable African Americans to secure economic self-reliance, parity, power and civil rights. Jewel Jones worked tirelessly and his efforts were profound. He continued to lead the organization until 1941 in which his successor, Lester B. Granger took over.

"I remember when I was over the NUL and we had accomplished so much. At the same time, I felt that I was at a point where it would be beneficial for me to appoint a successor. My health wasn't what it once was and I needed to rest. When the time came for me to transition out of the leadership position, I selected an Alpha man to take over. Brother Lester Blackwell Granger became the Executive Director to replace me. There goes another Alpha man!"

"Wow!" Howard says.

"In Brother Granger's first year in charge, he began working with the organizers of the famous March on Washington. We all know that our dear and beloved brother Dr. Martin Luther King Jr. delivered the most powerful speech given in American history at that march. Alpha men are always first, always the leaders and always the outstanding components to any organization or event. Our good brother Lester remained at the helm of the League for twenty years."

"Twenty years!" Wil proclaims. His proclamation is

more of emphasis than surprise.

"Yes, until 1961 when he selected a successor. As I did, he looked no further than his own fraternity brothers in making his selection. Alpha Phi Alpha brother Whitney M. Young Jr. became his replacement and took over the National Urban League in 1961."

"Stop spoiling my fun!" Jewel Tandy blurts out.

"Excuse me?" Jewel Jones responds to Vertner's interruption.

"That's the Alpha brother that I was going to speak on as to who I am impressed with and now you're spoiling it!" Jewel Tandy laughs.

"My apologies brother, I didn't know you were going to speak on Brother Young."

"I jest Kinckle. Proceed with your accolades. I'll choose another brother."

"Oh no, please. I insist. Speak on the brother whom you wish."

"We're talking about Alpha men. I have a thousand to choose from because there are a thousand I've been impressed with. Please, continue. Brother Whitney was critical to the National Urban League and you of all people need to speak on that." Jewel Tandy concedes.

"Thank you my brother. I appreciate that." Jewel Jones continues.

"I love that. We have so many brothers to choose from." Gregory says. "We can do this all day."

"We really can." Denny adds. "There's no question there."

"Yes but we won't brothers! I've had enough midnight meetings with you gents to last me a lifetime and another!" Jewel Tandy says.

"Wholeheartedly concur!" Jewel Kelley adds.

"I will continue with my good brother Whitney Young and try not to be long winded." Jewel Jones promises. Jewel Eugene Kinckle Jones has always been known to be an eloquent speaker. What he has not been known as is a brief one. Maybe that will change today. "When I consider the work of Brother Young, I have to say to myself that he is extraordinary yet a typical Alpha man. I remember being in this very house with these brothers assembled here and talking about what we wanted our fraternity to be. We talked about the Negro students who may come after us from different walks of life and what the makeup of their character would be. If I could build an Alpha man from every aspect of what I wanted him to be, in the end, he would be named Whitney Moore Young Jr. When Brother Lester turned control of the League over to Brother Young, the National Urban League had thirty eight employees. By our standards at that time, that was good. Brother Young took those thirty eight employees and turned it into sixteen hundred!"

"Wow!" Denny proclaims.

"That is quite a turnaround." Brother Harris states. "I'm very familiar with the work of Whitney Young. He made monumental strives on behalf of the National Urban League and our people in general."

"Yes indeed he did my brother historian!" Jewel Jones continues with even more excitement in his voice. "The annual budget was $325,000. He turned that into $6,100,000! This is a phenomenal brother that I am proud to call an Alpha man! Not only did he represent the League well which you all know is dear to my heart but he was the third representative of Alpha Phi Alpha to lead the organization into greater heights and deeper depths. I salute him today as one of the men who I am absolutely impressed with as a brother."

"That is so impressive! I'm proud to call him brother as Brother Sean stated earlier. To call these men brother is an honor!" Kagi chimes in.

"You're right but you also have to think that someone is going to say to call you a brother is an honor some day! What legacy are you going to leave? How will you make the Jewels and all of us proud of you young brother?" Sean McCaskill's question is posed to Kagi but can be taken in and answered by anyone in the room. It is more for thought than to literally be answered.

"And that still isn't all of what I have to share. There's so much more to Brother Whitney Young and what he was able to accomplish." Jewel Jones continues. "Did you brothers know that our brother was an advisor to three different presidents?"

"I actually didn't know that Brother Jewel founder!" Donald says. That surprises most brothers as Donald Ross knows more Alpha history than most.

"President Kennedy, President Johnson and President Nixon were all advised by Whitney Young. President Johnson awarded our brother the highest award a civilian can receive. He received the Presidential Medal of Freedom in 1969."

"I see why you're so impressed with these brothers. I see why you all are extremely impressed." Kagi says.

"Yes indeed! Very impressed with the list of brothers you have mentioned dear founders!" Brother Harris states.

"Allow me to impress you further regarding our brother Whitney! Do you brothers have any idea how many monuments in this country are named after this great Alpha man who was my successor? The East Capitol Street Bridge in Washington, DC was renamed the Whitney Young Memorial Bridge. There is a museum erected in his birthplace of Kentucky which is an historic landmark. Kentucky State University has a School of Honors and Liberal Studies that is named after him. Clark Atlanta University named its School of Social Work after him. The Boy Scouts of America created the Whitney M. Young Jr. Service Award. The African American MBA Association at The Wharton School at the University of Pennsylvania began an annual Whitney M. Young Jr. Memorial

Conference. That conference is now the longest student run conference at The Wharton School. There is a Whitney Young High School in both Chicago and Cleveland. There is a Whitney Young Elementary school in Dallas. There is a Whitney Young Health Center in Albany, NY. Lastly, there is a United States postage stamp that our brother was honored with as part of the Black Heritage series. So to say that I am impressed with our brother Whitney M. Young Jr. is an understatement. A great Alpha man indeed! Not only him but all of the brothers who were participants of the Urban League. Marc, Lester and Whitney and the countless number of Alphas who worked in some capacity for the League. I thank these brothers from the bottom of my heart for carrying the mantle of what was started so long ago. They have taken it up so many levels and I am forever proud and indebted."

"That was heartfelt Jewel Jones. You've given me a new perspective on all of these brothers." Julian says. "Thank you for opening my eyes to the accomplishments of these great leaders."

"Me too. It feels so good to be an Alpha man." Donald says.

"Excellent breakdown and very educational!" Brother McCaskill is next to chime in. "See, we need to make sure every young brother knows this information. We need to make sure our oral tradition is passed down griot style. Every Alpha needs to hear this. Every brother needs to have that one Alpha that they consider to be either a mentor or someone they would like to aspire to be! I love this!"

"Speaking of that brother Regional Vice President, who would be an Alpha that you're impressed with? Just because you just spoke up." Jewel Tandy breaks rank and throws the question to a brother who is not a founding Jewel.

Brother Sean accepts the challenge of answering the question. "Personally, I'm so impressed with our 31st General President Brother Harry Johnson. Brother Johnson was selfless and he dedicated so much in the raising of funds through contributions for the King Memorial in DC. That was outstanding work that only an Alpha man could accomplish!"

"Of course Harry is a personal friend of mine and a great brother. You're speaking right Brother McCaskill. He put all he had into that project and when I tell you that he worked tirelessly day and night to reach our goals, I am not kidding. He ate, slept, and breathed the King Memorial project. He is an excellent example of an Alpha who we all should be modeled after. Great answer brother Sean." Brother Darryl Matthews succeeded Brother Johnson as the 32nd General President and knows Brother Johnson well.

"Did you brothers know... watch this, that there have only been two African American men in the history of this country to raise over 100 million dollars for any single particular project?" Brother McCaskill asks.

"Really? Jewel Callis asks.

"In the history of the country?" I ask as well. I never knew this.

Brother McCaskill responds. "In the history of the United States of America, there have only been two Black men who have raised over 100 million dollars for any single project. Our brother, Harry Johnson, is one of those Black men! He raised over 100 million for the Dr. King Memorial. The other is President Barack Obama! Now tell me Alphas aren't in good company!"

"Damn! Now that's good knowledge to know!" Howard proclaims. "Good shit!"

"Wow! I'm floored!" Denny says.

"The greatness that is our organization is astounding! We have greatness in our house! We have since our beginning. It is evidenced by the seven jewels among us and in the many brothers who followed in their footsteps." Brother Harris describes the greatness of the fraternity by linking the founders with the great men of Alpha who followed.

"Jewel Tandy, you're the only Jewel who hasn't spoken on the Alpha brother who most impressed you. Do you want to now?" I ask.

"I was going to submit Whitney Young but since Kinck took him, I'll mention an even greater Alpha." Jewel Tandy responds to my invitation to continue the topic. "I submit to the brotherhood a great Alpha, Vertner W. Tandy!"

Everyone in the room laughs. I'm not sure if he is

joking. I assume he is since he is laughing with us.

"We'd love to hear you speak on yourself Jewel Tandy!" Kagi states.

"No no, I'm much too modest for that."

"Since when?" Jewel Murray looks at Jewel Tandy with a look on his face suggesting he doesn't believe him at all.

"How about I do Brother DuBois. Does that please the brotherhood?"

"Certainly!" I say with a smile.

"He's definitely one of our premier brothers who we all can admire. It would not be out of the realm of possibilities for an Alpha man to select W.E.B. Dubois as an Alpha brother that he is impressed with." Jewel Tandy states definitively. "So let's begin shall we? William Edward Burghardt is his name and the interesting thing about him, to me at least, is that he was organizing as we were organizing."

"What do you mean?" Brother Gayle asks.

"He was the founder, or one of the founders of an event known as the Niagara Movement. It was a movement to come against desegregation. They met in July 1905. We arrived on campus 2 months later. After we met one another, we began to organize our literary society and this thing took form. Many of our discussions back then centered around the theology of DuBois and the Niagara Movement and my mentor,

Booker Washington. They had opposing views on things. Both were respected, yet had differing opinions on how to do the same thing."

"Fascinating!" Julian states.

"Truly is!" Brother McCaskill chimes in.

"Yes brothers it is." Jewel Tandy continues. "Along the lines of what my other Jewel founders stated, Alphas are first in much of what we do. In the same fashion, Brother DuBois was the first Black man to earn a doctorate degree at Harvard University. How many brothers knew that bit of Black history?"

I didn't.

"I didn't know that." Denny says.

"I didn't know that either." Darryl says.

"Neither did I." Sean Gayle says.

"I'm learning all kinds of stuff!" Howard states.

"We're all familiar with the NAACP. He was one of the co-founders. Look at the size of the organization today and the work they've done over the decades. He was the brainchild of that. An Alpha man!" Jewel Tandy continues.

"Yes sir! The organization that we know today as the NAACP originated with the Niagara Movement." Brother Harris states. "The Niagara Movement, as I believe, was a bit more radical than the NAACP. There were only African Americans that took part of the Niagara Movement whereas two Europeans helped found the NAACP. Their approach to finding a solution to the problems of the Negro race were quite different so there was a splitting if you will. Many of the members overlapped between the two organizations but once the Niagara Movement ceased, the NAACP began to grow. It obviously continues to this day." Bob Harris is a walking history book as is Donald Ross. Both brothers have a vast knowledge of African American history as well as Alpha history. To sit with either of the two of them is both educational and enlightening. To sit with the two of them and the Jewel founders of Alpha is almost overwhelming.

"What I find interesting," right on time is Donald with a phrase that he often uses when discussing history; what I find interesting, "is that Jewel Vertner Woodson Tandy would suggest Brother DuBois as one of his favorite Alphas yet was a student and proponent of one of DuBois' most staunch critics in Booker T. Washington."

"Well wait brother, I never said that DuBois was my favorite Alpha. My favorite Alpha is Vertner Woodson Tandy!"

Brothers laugh, especially Donald who made the statement.

"Let's make sure we are all on one accord brothers. My favorite Jewel is me!"

'Duly noted my jewel." Donald says still laughing.

Jewel Tandy smiles as he continues. "Let me say this. We have always held a somewhat..." he searches for the right phrase, "difference of opinion on the means to correct the same problem. If there is a problem and we're all trying to find a solution, and the solution is ten, how many different number combinations can we use to get to ten? Is any particular directive wrong? Not as long as it solves the problem. DuBois and Washington had different directives to solve the same problem. Now they were vastly different but they still addressed the same problem."

"That's an interesting way to put it." Wil states.

"We were in college, young and impressionable. He was establishing greatness for our community. We had heard of him. The honor to us is when we approached him about honorary membership. He accepted our offer and was very impressed with Alpha Phi Alpha! That was a shining moment for us! That was a moment we all will remember and appreciate. One thing I appreciate about Brother DuBois is that he was so controversial. I love that. Not the norm at all and I can respect that. I'll end with this point... there's an interesting Alpha moment that most people don't know about. I don't know if brothers of Alpha even know. During the March on Washington, both of the Alpha brothers that we mentioned were speakers. Brother Whitney Young spoke and of course Dr. Martin King Jr. spoke. Well, before Dr. King spoke, Whitney approached him. When they hugged one another, they exchanged the fraternal handshake. While doing so, Whitney whispered in Martin's ear that Brother W.E.B. Dubois had passed away the day before. A moment of silence was observed from the entire crowd of over 200,000 people when it was announced. A fitting tribute for a great Alpha man! That's all I got brothers. I hope I answered the question adequately."

"Brother Jewel Tandy, and to all of you, you did an excellent job in answering the brother's question! I feel I can speak for all the bros here that it's enlightening and impressive to hear your thoughts on Alphas you think are special. The house is blessed, I know that for a fact!" I say that while containing my emotion. It is a beautiful thing to hear Black men speak about the greatness of brotherhood. We could easily talk about the ills of our society, our community, or even the chapters that make up the fraternity. Instead, the meeting has steered in the direction of upward.

"Oh, and one more note! If I may." Jewel Tandy adds.

"Please oblige us with more Jewel Tandy." I say.

"DuBois' only daughter Yolande married a brother of Alpha Phi Alpha. He was a pretty well-known Alpha as he was a poet of the Harlem Renaissance. You brothers may have heard of him. Brother Countee Cullen."

"Countee Cullen is my favorite poet! I love his work! I didn't know he married W.E.B. DuBois' daughter!" I say. I've been a fan of Brother Countee Cullen for many years. I've read the poets of the Harlem Renaissance and fell in love with Cullen's work before I knew he was an Alpha. His mastery of the rhythm of a poem is to be admired. I remember pulling out some of his work during the riots in Baltimore when Freddie Gray was killed by the police. There was a poem that Countee Cullen wrote that was eerily prophetic of that time. It was, 'Once riding in old Baltimore, heart-filled, head-filled with glee... I saw a Baltimorean keep looking straight at me... Now I was eight and very small, and he was no whit bigger... and so I smiled, but he poked out his tongue, and called me, 'Nigger.'... I saw the whole of Baltimore from May until December... Of all the things that happened there that's all that I remember.' I have admired Brother Cullen's work for years and never knew who his wife was! "Thank you for that last bit of information about Brother DuBois! I'm sure we've all learned something!"

"Bruh!" Sean Gayle says so much in that one word.

"Brother Countee was one of my best friends." Jewel Jones says. "I used to joke with him frequently and say that he had mastered the art of singing without music."

Jewel Jones speaks often of his best friends who both were poets. Alpha brother Countee Cullen and Omega Psi Phi Fraternity member Langston Hughes were his best friends. Both were world renowned and greatly respected for their literary contributions during the Harlem Renaissance.

"Brother Gourdine, I'd like to ask the Jewels, or one of the Jewels a question." Brother McCaskill speaks right as I finish my comment and Sean Gayle responds.

"Sure sands! Go ahead." I respond.

"Thanks good brother. Jewel brothers, can you tell us your thoughts on retention and reclamation? It seems as if it's always a topic of discussion among the brothers. As I ran for the various offices I ran for, I answered the questions many times. How can we reclaim brothers? How do we retain brothers? How do we go back and get disenfranchised brothers? So I would like to know what challenges you may have faced in your era and how did you work through it."

"Excellent question Brother Sean and I'll answer." Jewel Murray speaks first. "I would say this to brothers who have left the fold. Brothers in Alpha Phi Alpha, if this means anything, and if the vows when you were initiated into the mysteries of Alpha Phi Alpha mean anything to you, you should make every effort within yourself to stage a 100 percent comeback. Once a brother in Alpha Phi Alpha, always a brother in Alpha Phi Alpha. Does not the spirit of old APA still beat strong enough within you to make you want to take advantage of this special opportunity to align yourself with the nearest graduate chapter or undergraduate chapter? You owe it to your former brothers, you owe it to your chapter to help them make a 100 percent drive in staging this comeback. Does not the old spirit of Alpha Phi Alpha ring in your ears as it did in your college days? Brothers in Alpha Phi Alpha, we need you, we need your assistance in carrying out our great constructive program. We need you to prove to the world at large that Alpha Phi Alpha is not only the first Negro College Fraternity, but it is also the strongest and the largest of all the College Fraternities among Negroes."

"Wow, well said Jewel Murray!" Sean McCaskill says.

"Yeah, that was very well said!" Kagi says.

Jewel Chapman speaks next. "Just as I have obtained one of the most cherished memories of my life through participation in this brotherly venture, so will I have the greatest disappointment of my life if I should see this organization lose sight of the principles that it has always maintained, and no longer stand for the beautiful and the ethical in the life of those who have been admitted to its ranks as well as those who see in this organization one of the most remarkable and enriching features of our Negro collegiate life. Your memories are your reason. Share with the wayward brothers and remind them of their memories."

"Our main purpose in 1906 was to found a fraternity composed of groups of undergraduates so chosen in the various colleges and universities that they would represent the best of the Negro youth of that institution, banded together to help each other in the various essentials necessary for success in college; successful scholarship, healthful recreation and clean living. After completing the college course, we hoped that they would continue their bonds of brotherhood, not like Jacob and Esau, but rather according to the mystical story of Damon and Pythias."

"George, if I may, you might want to explain the story

of Damon and Pythias if there are any young brothers in the room not familiar with the legend." Jewel Tandy says in response to Jewel Kelley's statement.

"Right. Let me not assume. The story of Damon and Pythias is a legend surrounding the Pythagorean ideal of friendship. Pythias is accused and charged of creating a plot against the tyrannical Dionysius II of Syracuse. Pythias makes a request of Dionysius II that he be allowed to settle his affairs on the condition that he leaves his friend, Damon, as a hostage. The agreement was if Pythias did not return, Damon would be executed in his stead. Eventually, Pythias returns to face execution to the amazement of Dionysius, who because of the sincere trust and love of their friendship, then lets both Damon and Pythias go free."

"Wow, I had never heard of that story before!" I say.

"Would you come back for me bruh?" Sean Gayle asks me.

"Bruh, you my boy from Beta and from Jersey but um..." My refusal to complete the sentence indicates I would not come back to save Sean Gayle. Clearly I'm joking as is indicated by the smile on my face. Everyone begins to laugh.

"I hate bros." Sean says. This causes brothers to laugh even the more.

"Thank you Jewel Kelley. Anyone else want to comment on reclamation? These responses are great!" I say.

"Yes these responses are invaluable to us!" Denny says. "In his role as Director of Membership Services, these words are invaluable as he considers programs that would encourage brothers to actively continue their participation in the fraternity.

"Any other Jewel brother care to respond to the question?" I ask.

"Yes sir, I'd like to." Jewel Ogle says. "Never before was it as incumbent upon every member to restate loyalty and exemplify fraternal obligation by consistent life and unimpeachable character. But these must now be reinforced by a growing consciousness of the responsibilities that Alpha Phi Alpha faces in the world today. Where if ever the problems which beset us are to be solved and a way of deliverance discovered, it must be by the application of those principles upon which we are founded."

"Let me ask a question stemming from this topic. I've traveled throughout the various chapters of specifically the East and I hear a common question concerning a lot of brothers. Many brothers have a hard time convincing their line brothers or prophytes or even younger brothers to remain active in the fraternity. They find themselves in debates trying to get a brother to come back to the fold. Some brothers may have legitimate life issues that prevent them from active participation but many brothers make excuses. What would you, as one of the founders, say to a brother who is choosing to remain inactive?" Sean McCaskill asks a question that I am sure most Alphas in the room has heard at least once.

"Yeah and one brother even told me he was an ex Alpha! I was like what the hell? Once an Alpha always an Alpha! Or so my prophytes taught me!" Howard says.

Jewel Callis immediately responds. "When you address yourself as an ex Alpha, you make it impossible for me to be of any service to you. You make yourself an expatriate or a back slider. Alpha Phi Alpha is made up of the spiritual qualities of men. Error lives on the frailties of men. In a democratic society, error can be corrected from the inside only."

"Preach!" Sean McCaskill encourages.

"Take steps immediately to return to Alpha. When you can address me as Brother Jewel, then we can discuss your grievances, supported by evidence. Only then can I help you."

"Wow!" Denny's one word speaks volumes and renders the rest of us speechless for a moment.

"Okay brothers, I'm gonna take another question from one of our brothers who submitted on Twitter. This one is from @lesstlouis and his question is... 'To each of the Jewels, name one thing about yourself that brothers may not already know'.

"Oh this should be good." Sean Gayle says.

"I'll start." Jewel Jones begins. "Have any of you heard of President Franklin D. Roosevelt's Black

Cabinet?"

No one responds.

"Right. I didn't think any of you would have heard of it. The Black Cabinet was a group that President Roosevelt put together of Blacks who were in public policy. The group was set up to offer him advice on a variety of subjects that he may not be well versed in. I was a member of that cabinet. I don't know if many Alpha brothers know that about me but I would assume that they do not."

"Wow, great answer Jewel Jones. I certainly didn't know that." Sean Gayle states.

"Don't think I knew that either." Denny responds next.

"I believe I'd read that somewhere." Donald states.

"Me too." Gregory states.

"I knew that too Brother Jewel Jones." Brother Harris informs us that he was aware. No one is surprised that Donald or Brother Harris probably knew. Gregory as well.

"What was the Black Cabinet?" Kagi asks.

"Well it wasn't called that at first. At first it was called The Federal Council of Negro Affairs. At that time, Negros didn't have adequate representation in the government on any level. Especially in the South where many of our people couldn't or wouldn't vote. The president and first lady presented the concept to a select group of prominent Blacks to join the Council to try to right the imbalance. We were a think tank to educate the office of the president and all of government on the needs of our people. Policies were put in place but more importantly, people were put in place. Government agencies were beginning to be headed by members of our community and that opened the door to the best and brightest to come in and lead. There had never in the past been so many Blacks chosen to work together for the betterment of our community so we took full advantage."

"Who were some of the other members of The Black Cabinet Jewel Jones?" Wil asks.

"Most prominent was Mary McLeod Bethune. She was friends with First Lady Eleanor Roosevelt and a strong advocate for civil rights. She'd be the one you brothers would probably be most familiar with. Some of the other members, let me think." Jewel Jones looks toward the ceiling as he remembers some of the members of The Black Cabinet. "Edgar Brown, Henry Hunt, Alfred Smith, John Whitten. They all were executive leaders of government agencies."

"That's fascinating Brother Jones, thank you so much for sharing that." I state. "Anyone else wish to answer the question from the brother online on Twitter?"

"I don't know if many of you know that I served as First Master of the Mt. Moriah Lodge No. 25 in Troy New York." states Jewel Kelley. "I also served as District Deputy Grandmaster of the Grand Lodge of the State of New York and 33$^{rd}$ degree Mason of Utica Consitory of Scottish Rites."

"I too am a double brother as I was a national officer for the Benevolent Protective Order of the Elks." Jewel Ogle chimes in. "I don't know if many brothers are aware of that fact."

General President Darryl Matthews comments "Brother Jewel, do you have the pass? I'm Northstar number 1, Free and Accepted Mason, Prince Hall Affiliated. Chicago, Illinois.

Denny adds, "I was raised at Jones Creek Lodge number 833, Livingston, Alabama. I'm currently affiliated with the Roscoe C. Cartwright Lodge number 129 in Accokeek, Maryland."

As soon as Denny finishes his statement, Jewel Murray continues with the question that was asked. "I don't know if many brothers know that my mother taught music at Howard University. She was a pioneer in the fight for early education and there may not have been kindergarten education in Washington DC had it not been for my mother. Not at that time at least."

"Wow, can you elaborate on that Jewel Brother Murray? What do you mean by there may not have been kindergarten?" Sean Gayle asks.

"Mother dedicated her life to establishing free kindergartens through DC. She trained kindergarten teachers as well. She lobbied Congress and was awarded $12,000 to establish kindergarten classes. Those funds went a long way in 1898 so she was successful in implanting the schools and many programs. She lobbied Congress again in the great year of 1906 and continued her work by receiving more funds for the cause. One thing I always remember her saying was a quote that her mother told her. Mother would say 'Education is a pearl of great price by which you will be able to set yourself free in your environment, whatever that may be.' I'm sure most Alphas brothers wouldn't know that I come from a family that was dedicated to education. Even my father who worked for the Library of Congress was a well-respected bibliographer."

"What were their names?" Brother Kagi asks. "Your parents I mean."

"My mother's name is Anna and my father is Daniel Murray. My father submitted over 500 books written by Black authors for an exhibit in the Negro authorship section of the Paris World Exposition. I bet not many brothers know that either."

"I didn't even know that!" Jewel Tandy says as he looks at Jewel Murray who is seated to his left. Murray smiles at Vertner's comment.

"As I mentioned, many brothers don't know."

"That's a great fact Jewel Murray." Donald states.

"Thank you. I appreciate that."

"Does any other founder wish to answer this question before we move on?" I ask.

"I'll attempt to come up with something that brothers may not know." Jewel Chapman speaks up. I'm a little surprised that he chose this question to answer but I believe it makes sense. He's a very quiet person so I'm surprised at his willingness to share. At the same time, there were many years that he was unaccounted for after he left Cornell University. There may be many things that he accomplished during that time that we aren't aware of. He continues. "I don't think most brothers know that I have a love for poetry and I used to write poems."

"Wow, I didn't know that good brother!" Brother Harris states.

"Me neither!" Donald says with a smile. "Care to share a piece with us?"

All eyes turn on Jewel Chapman as he attempts to remembersomethingthathewrote. "Letmeremember." He pauses before he begins. "Just to be a friend of yours and to know you're one of mine...With a friendship that endures and grows sweeter like old wine... Just to clasp you by the hand in a friendly sort of way... and to know you understand all the things I want to say." He stops. That is either the entire poem, all he can remember, or all he cares to share. In either case, the brothers are appreciative as they clap for him.

"Very nice good sir. Well done." Jewel Callis commends his fellow Jewel, Chapman.

After graduating from Cornell University, several years had passed with no communication from Jewel

Chapman. It had reached a point where the general consensus was that he had passed away. His name was listed as having entered Omega Chapter before he reappeared alive and well. He had spent his time in Tallahassee at Florida A&M University.

"I'll add to the question." Jewel Tandy says. "I believe the brotherhood knows that I'm an architect. They should know at least that. Most probably have heard that my most famous work was the home of Madam C.J. Walker. Well, after she died, the home went through a few owners until it was finally declared a national historic landmark. So the house is probably more famous than many people realize."

"Jewel Vertner how large is the house?" Wil asks.

"The home is 20,000 square feet. A proper size estate. I remember it well. I'm not certain I answered the question accordingly. That wasn't so much a fact about me as it was a fact about something I accomplished."

"And that's what makes it an excellent answer to the question Jewel brother!" Donald states with a smile.

"Yes indeed." Denny adds.

"Thanks for sharing. That's good to know and like you said, I'm sure most brothers don't know that. Maybe except Brother Harris." Everyone looks at Brother Harris who simply smiles which acknowledges that he probably knew.

"Alright brothers, let's move to the next question.

Brother Franklin, you mentioned that you had a question for the Jewels. What's your question?" I ask as I pat Howard on the shoulder.

"Thanks Brother Gourdine. I do have a question and this might cause you to laugh but I wanna know something. If each of you could give a line name to a different Jewel, what would that line name be and why."

"What? Oh wow this is gonna be hilarious!" Sean Gayle laughs as he responds to Howard's question.

"Oh yeah, great question bro!" Sean McCaskill responds as well.

"Wow. Line names huh?" Jewel Kelley says.

"You'd be Mr. President huh George?" Jewel Tandy says with a smile. The other Jewels smile and Jewel Callis laughs. Their smiles indicate the name for Jewel George is fitting and appropriate.

"I suppose so." Jewel George says. What about you Vertner? Or Gene? What names would suit yourselves?"

"I'd definitely call Gene something Egyptian like a lot of brothers do." Jewel Murray says.

"Babatunde."

"What?" Jewel Murray asks Jewel Jones what name he just blurted out.

Jewel Jones responds. "Babatunde. It means return

of the father. My father was a professor and an expert on Egyptian mythology, language and culture. When I returned from Cornell, I brought Alpha Phi Alpha home with me. I brought it to Howard University and to Virginia Union University. My father was so impressed that I had returned home with something substantial that he became a brother. My son had always been impressed with the fraternity and he became a brother. So the name, to me at least, is fitting. If I could select my own line name, that's probably what I would select."

"I think I'd like to be known as Hell Freezer!" Jewel Tandy declares. Everyone laughs.

"And why is that my brother?" Howard asks.

"You remember my famous line, 'We must fight til hell freezes over and then fight on the ice!' I remember saying that in 1937 and those sentiments hold true today. If anybody is ready to fight for the character of this organization, it's me. I'll fight for manly deeds and scholarship. I'll fight for the old gold and black. For the shield and all it represents! Call me Hell Freezer because I'll fight on this here ice!"

"I might as soon call you Hell Raiser!" Jewel Ogle says as he laughs.

Jewel Vertner can't help but to laugh at what his fellow Jewel founder says, as do the others, as do us all. It's so interesting to see the interactions of the founders. These men have been through so much during their years at Cornell and the stages of their lives afterward.

The bond that was created on the campus in 1905 and 1906 caused an affect that no one living can describe. Due to the actions of these seven men, hundreds of thousands of people have joined Black Greek letter organizations. Before there was a Black Greek letter fraternity, there was these seven students. Before there was a Black Greek letter sorority, there was these seven students. Would these organizations have been founded if these seven students had not founded Alpha first? Maybe. We'll never know because factual history states the seven founded Alpha first. Such a debt is owed to these seven by every young man who has had aspirations to become an Alpha man and then been privileged enough to enter the House of Alpha. Now we observe casual conversation amongst them and it is a brotherly joy to witness.

"I think I would give Charles The Silent Sphinx." Jewel Callis states. "There's a power behind men who speak little but say much."

"I'd give him Business Minded. For you to own two businesses while maintaining classes and establishing a fraternity is remarkable. I don't know how you did it and I was there to witness it." Jewel Olge says.

"Likewise Bob. I can say the same for you. How many students were able to marry the love of their life and have a baby while maintaining classes and found a fraternity? Not many I would assume." Jewel Chapman responds.

"So we should give Robert the line name Father Pharaoh." Jewel Tandy says.

"It is fitting." Jewel Jones says.

"I appreciate that brothers." Jewel Ogle responds with a smile.

"I have a question. What are you brothers' line names?" Jewel Callis asks.

"And what are the meanings behind them? I love to hear the meanings behind some of these creative names." Jewel Jones adds.

"I guess I'll go first since I asked the question." Howard says. "My line name is FUPAME which is an acronym for... y'all brothers excuse my French..."

"Say it bro!" Sean encourages Brother Howard.

"You sure about that Brother Gayle?" Wil says laughing. The brothers laugh as Howard continues.

"It's an acronym for Fuck You Pay Me." Brother Howard says matter factly.

"What!" Donald says.

"I got the name for two reasons. As y'all know, I play in a band and I used to make the big brothers wait for our set to begin until I got there. I was always playing club dates at the time we were to meet. Then once my gig was over, I wouldn't leave the club until I got my money! So brothers got mad at me because they had to start late. Plus brothers recognized that I got the kind of personality where I ain't goin' nowhere. Once brothers realized those two things, they gave me that line name." That name suits Howard Franklin perfectly! I laugh to myself because I am familiar with some of his prophytes. Aldean Pearson and Jeff Sellers were at Double O Chapter when I was at Beta Chapter. I remember Big Eddie Reed too. These brothers were instrumental in bringing in Howard Franklin and I know they're proud of him.

"My line name is Shai." I say. "It means personification of destiny or fate. More specifically, there was a scene in the Egyptian mystery systems where a man would weigh his heart against a feather. If his heart was too heavy and he carried too many issues, he would be put to death. There were two entities, male and female who oversaw the scales for the heart vs the feather. The male entity was named Shai. So one of my big brothers felt that I was destined to be successful in life and he gave me that name."

"I like that!" says Jewel Jones enthusiastically.

"Darrius' line name became the name of a popular singing group. Two of his line brothers and one of his prophytes from 1989 formed a group and they used his line name. They were insanely popular and traveled the world." Sean Gayle says. Sean was there when Shai took off and became a music sensation in the 1990s. He is all too familiar with the story of the group using my name and making it internationally known. Shai member Marc Gay is the prophyte from 1989 who gave me the line name. My line brothers Carl Martin and Darnell VanRensalier are the other two brothers in the group. I've always been honored that they used my line name and gained huge success with it.

"Very creative." Jewel Murray says. "Please, go on."

Darryl Matthews, the past General President, speaks next. "I was on a solo ship. The S.S. Polymorphic Plebian. It means that I went through many changes as a common man to become and Alpha man."

"Awesome!" Jewel Kelley says.

"I'm greatly appreciating these responses and names." Jewel Murray states.

"Hannibal is my line name. The Carthaginian general Hannibal was one of the greatest military leaders in history. His most famous campaign took place during the Second Punic War when he caught the Romans off guard by crossing the Alps. The brothers called me that because I was a leader on the football field and a leader on campus." Sean McCaskill adds.

"And a leader in Alpha Phi Alpha." Jewel Callis adds with a smile. What a statement; to have a founding Jewel consider you a leader. Sean is visually appreciative.

"Thank you Jewel Calllis. I work hard and do my best to encourage and enlighten my brothers at every opportunity."

"You live up to your line name then." Jewel Callis continues.

"He does! That's a good brother right there!" Howard says confidently.

"I'll go next." Sean Gayle says. "My line name is Tehuti which means Egyptian god or angel of wisdom. Tehuti won't communicate with you unless you ask him a question. Then he writes his answers down slowly and carefully so they resonate. He doesn't speak because actions speak louder than words."

"Wooo whooo! Yes! I love it! Now that's what I'm talking about!" Howard exclaims. "That's tight bro!"

"I like that too!" Donald says. "I love that explanation. I received the name Dr. Jekyll. My line brother was aptly named Mr. Hyde." Donald states. "My line brother actually named us. I was about to be Dr. Ross and the brothers were trying to figure out how I knew so much information. So he called me a doctor because of my vast knowledge. There were only two of us on line so naturally he became Mr. Hyde. My line brother is John Haynes."

"My line name is Akhenaton because he was a family-oriented pharaoh, and while I was on line I often talked about my family. Also, he was known as Amenophis IV, and I was a number 4 on line." Gregory says. "Howard this was a great question. I'm glad you asked. I'm really curious to hear the rest of the Jewels name themselves."

Kagi responds next. "My line name is L'ınsolent. It's French for the insubordinate one. It's a tribute to my French African roots and a reflection of my spirit as an ambitious self-starter. My entire line is named Tendaji. It's Swahili for makes things happen because we came from different walks in life and different backgrounds in order to come together as one under Alpha."

"Good stuff Brother." Wil says. "I got my line name after I crossed. Well, I got one during line but I'm not sharing that!"

"Share it bro! Share it!" Howard says loudly.

"As I said," the brothers laugh at how Wil dismisses Howard, "I'm not sharing that. After I crossed, they called me Iceberg and that's my line name."

"That's deep." Sean McCaskill says. "An iceberg looks one size when you first glance at it but its depth is unknown until you look under some layers!"

Wil nods at Sean as if to agree with his definition of an iceberg.

"I wonder what the Jewel founders would name their line." Kagi says.

"Their line?" I ask.

"Yeah. The seven of them."

"How about..." Jewel Tandy pauses, "...The Seven Jewels."

Everyone laughs from Jewel Tandy's response. Kagi probably laughs the loudest. The response is in no way sarcastic to his question. It is more stating the obvious in a comical way.

"That definitely fits my Jewel!" Kagi says smiling.

]Denny adds his answer to the question. "I actually have two. I got one on the night that I went over but I don't care for that one too much. Long story about that." Denny laughs. "But the one that I'm more known for is Shuga' Bear. I like that one a lot better anyway."

"It fits you big guy!" I say.

"You know it good brother!" Denny smiles back at me. Denny has been like a big brother to me for several years. I was a member of the Omicron Lambda Alpha Chapter in Washington DC under Denny's administration. He served the brotherhood with four consecutive terms as chapter president. Under his leadership, the chapter grew to numbers they hadn't seen in years.

"Okay, how about you Jewel Murray. Got any suggestions for any of your fellow Jewel brothers?" Howard continues with his question.

Jewel Murray rubs his chin as if he is in deep thought. "Line names for my brothers. Let's see. For Henry, I would definitely call him The Timekeeper. Henry is the most punctual brother I know."

"Yes! That's it! Perfect for Henry!" Jewel Tandy says laughing. This is the loudest laugh he has let out this entire Town Hall Meeting.

Jewel Murray continues. "George I would give the name The Prize Fighter."

"Now that is appropriate!" Jewel Jones says about his friend George Kelley. I've seen that fighter spirit on many an occasion. Our meetings went well into the evening hours at times due to George's feisty attitude."

George agrees with this assessment with his smile.

Jewel Callis speaks up. "So we've all been named. The Prize Fighter, Father Figure, Babatunde, The Silent Sphinx, Hell Freezer," Jewel Callis laughs as he says Jewel Tandy's line name, "and I'm the Timekeeper. We only have Nathaniel left. What are our thoughts brothers?"

"I'd like to name him Nathaniel Alphadom Murray!" Jewel Tandy says. The entire room laughs as Vertner takes both hands to the air and opens them up slowly as he says Alphadom in a slow manner. His jest is comical and timely and causes everyone to burst in laughter.

"How about we give him an acronym like Brother Howard Franklin has." Jewel Chapman says.

"Okay like what?" I ask.

"How about B.M.L. and I will let one of you young brothers guess what each letter stands for." Jewel Chapman says with a smile.

"Black Man Lurking." Howard blurts out. Everyone laughs.

"No sir." Jewel Chapman states.

"Be More Loving." Denny says. Based on how Denny remarks, it seems clear that he is joking as well. Everyone laughs.

In a more serious tone, Brother Harris answers the riddle. "Beta Mu Lambda. The chapters that Jewel Murray had a hand in establishing. Beta Chapter and Mu Lambda Chapter." Of course the national historian would be able to decode the riddle by Jewel Charles Chapman.

"You're absolutely right brother. That is exactly what I had in mind." Jewel Chapman responds. "Good job figuring that out."

"Thank you sir." Brother Harris says.

"Thanks for that question Howard. That really was a good question that I never would've thought to ask." I congratulate Howard on an excellent question.

"You're welcome Brother Gourdine."

"Okay so, now that we all have line names, let's take another question from Twitter. This one comes from @walkerdl and his question is, 'To each Jewel founder, what is your favorite personal quote about Alpha Phi Alpha?'"

There is a pause before one of the Jewels answers. Jewel Murray answers first. "This was one of the passages of a speech that I gave at the General Convention in Ohio back in 1946. I spoke to the brotherhood and said don't get discouraged in your personal visits and efforts to rehabilitate brothers who will tell you yes in order to get rid of you and then fail to show up. All who are interested in the strayed brother or brothers should grasp this opportunity to put service before self. Go after that brother in your own auto or even hire a taxicab, if necessary, to impress him with the real need the local chapter has for his presence and influence. Expense should be nil, when the reward justifies the expense. For after all, what good is Alpha Phi Alpha to any of us if it does not teach us that as a servant of all, we must transcend all through service."

"That's awesome!" Denny says. "Well said and very timely to this day! The brothers need to hear that!"

"We must fight till hell freezes over and then fight on the ice." Jewel Tandy loudly proclaims the quote that many brothers are familiar with him saying. This may be his most familiar quote.

"You said that in December 1937." Donald says.

"You're right brother! I was fed up with some of the problems and issues Alpha Phi Alpha was having internally! I declared that I fought like hell to found this organization and some of the challenges we were facing at that time were uncalled for and avoidable. I couldn't stand it any longer. So I spoke out. I spoke out with everything that was in me. It was built in frustration but also grounded in love for this organization."

"It was well needed then and probably needed now." Wil states. If anyone would know the internal struggles we face as an organization, it would be Brother Lyle. He handles the business of Alpha like no one else. He equally understands the business like no one else.

Jewel Callis speaks next. "I remember saying the chief significance of Alpha Phi Alpha lies in its purpose to stimulate, develop and cement an intelligent, trained leadership in the unending fight for freedom, equality and fraternity. Our task is endless. That's probably my favorite quote."

"That was May 1946." Brother Harris speaks this time. The two historians, Brother Donald Ross and Brother Robert Harris are more than likely familiar with everything the Jewels said and did. Both men's knowledge of fraternity history is fascinating. It would be most useful for all brothers to converse with these historians and other brothers who are as knowledgeable of our fraternity's rich history.

"Let me see if I can think of something I said." Jewel Chapman says.

"Well while you're thinking, let me share this. I remember most of my statements. Alpha Phi Alpha, the oldest of Negro fraternities, with all of its members presumably far above the average American and having a good practical understanding of the salient factors involved in the Negro's problems, and which a membership upwards of eight thousand men, should be able to take into their hands the leadership in the Negro's struggle for status." Jewel Jones laughs as he shares this and explains why he laughs. "I said this in 1936. I can look at Alpha Phi Alpha today and we have added to that number twenty times yet the statement still remains. We need to be forefront minded at all times in our leadership efforts. Alpha Phi Alpha boasts some of the most identifiable leaders our race has seen in the industries of politics, business, religion, community development, entrepreneurism and athletics. There is a definite correlation between our ability to attract men of such caliber and our position as leaders in our communities."

"Well said." Darryl says. "I agree wholeheartedly!" he says enthusiastically. "I love when Alpha brothers are the leaders in industries. Makes me say there goes an Alpha man!"

"I love that too!" I add. I believe all members of fraternities and sororities have a bias when it comes to their own organizations. They love to see their fraternity brother or sorority sister achieve great things. We also hate to see images of our organizations with a negative light cast on them. Stories of hazing or other incidents where the law is broken or the university or chapter is embarrassed are always thorns in the side of our collective members. What Jewel Jones shared is relative to anyone in an organization. It rang true when he said it. It holds true today.

"I remember saying this." Jewel Chapman is ready to share a quote now. "I want you to understand that there never was or has been or will be, in the minds of the founders, including myself, the thought of any reward any notice coming to us for this experiment in brotherly cooperation and comradeship, which we initiated and which has developed, not necessarily because of any efforts of ours, into one of the best regarded organizations in the Negro collegiate world."

"That was very well put my brother!" Jewel Callis is the first Jewel to recognize another Jewel's quote.

"Thank you kind sir." Jewel Chapman responds with a smile.

"Anyone else wish to answer the brother's question from Twitter?" I ask.

"Yes. I do." Jewel Ogle says. "Never before was it as incumbent upon every member to restate loyalty and exemplify fraternal obligation by consistent life and unimpeachable character. I remember saying that."

"Such a great point!" Wil says. "That definitely could be said in today's Alpha."

"I finished that statement by saying but these must be reinforced by a growing consciousness of the responsibilities that Alpha Phi Alpha faces in the world today, where, if ever the problems which beset us are to be solved and a way of deliverance discovered, it must be by the application of those principles upon which we are founded. That was the entire statement and I still stand by those words." Jewel Ogle completes his quote.

"I'm so glad the brother submitted this question! This is a great question as well and I'm really enjoying the Jewels remembering these quotes that they made!" Howard says.

"Me too!" Denny adds. "Keep it up Jewel brothers. What else do you remember saying?"

Jewel Kelley is the final Jewel to quote himself. He begins promptly after being encouraged by Brother Johnson. "I wish to urge upon all the brothers the necessity for a broader bond of brotherhood in the communities where you reside. After allegiance to your God, family and country, let nothing shake your love for the fraternity and its ideas. Let every brother be truly a brother, promote his interest as if it was yours, and show to the world that Alpha Phi Alpha stands for more than mere words."

"December 1935!" Donald blurts out. Everyone laughs as well as Donald himself.

"Exactly right as I knew you would be my historian brother!" Jewel Kelley says.

"I've always appreciated you for that quote Jewel Kelley. That sums up so much of the way brothers should feel. That statement needs to be imbedded in the hearts and minds of every Alpha brother from young to old." Donald says. "I was hoping when the question was asked by the good brother from Twitter that you would state that as your quote."

"Well I've said so many things and I believe many are documented as historical record. I was obviously the first president of Alpha chapter so a lot of what I said was placed into archives and a historical keepsake. I obviously don't remember it all but I remember that statement and the sentiment behind it."

"Thank you gentlemen for answering that question. Let's keep the town hall meeting rolling right along. The next question for the Jewels or for any of you brothers who wish to answer deals with hazing. This is a topic often discussed with many different thoughts, opinions, angles, and viewpoints. So let's hear yours'. On the subject of hazing in general, what are your thoughts?

"I'm sure a lot of us if not all of us would like to respond to that question." Sean McCaskill says.

He's right.

"So who first?" I ask.

Before anyone can respond, Jewel Murray jumps at the chance to respond to this question. "Who has not heard of the so called Hell Week? Who has thought more than once of some way of reducing the brutalities and permanent physical injuries that many brothers have carried and will continue to carry to their graves? The first stages of the initiation are utterly brutal. I have stopped many a blindfold prospect from being beaten at the hands of an irresponsible Brother. The ceremonies as carried on in many chapters throughout the country were not the ceremonies that we planned or intended for brothers to use. This merciless brutality must he stopped! When Brother Eugene Kinckle Jones was initiated in ceremonies, in which I took part, there was no prolonged after effects in evidence. He can testify to that!"

"I was led away trembling however!" Jewel Jones says laughing. The room laughs with him which breaks the serious nature of Jewel Murray's response. Jewel Murray responds passionately in regard to the question. Without hesitation, he lets the brothers know how he feels.

"I agree with you Nate. I have seen men beaten so badly that three days later they could not walk." Jewel

Tandy says in a serious tone. This is probably the most serious I've seen him since the town hall meeting has begun. "None of us are in compliance with that type of behavior. None of us are in compliance with behavior detrimental to the health of a potential brother."

"Can you imagine what it was like to serve the greatest fraternity on Earth as General President and get phone calls from some of the most outlandish acts of violence one could imagine? We have put measures in place over the years to prevent these acts of violence. We have to be preventative instead of reactionary. This is how we will get to the point of eradicating it all for the love of Alpha." Darryl adds to the conversation.

"My initiation year was the last year of above ground pledging." Sean McCaskill states. "I remember the word going across that pledging was ending and the following year would be a totally different process."

"I crossed the same year." I add. I remember that as well. Sean McCaskill and I were on line at the same time, different chapters.

Brother McCaskill continues. "That was a pivotal time as the fraternity lead the charge to end hazing and these acts of violence forever. The General President at the time was Brother Henry Ponder. He was very vocal in recreating policy and procedures for Alpha. Alpha Phi Alpha was the first organization in the Pan Hel to eradicate pledging and change to a new process. The other organizations were soon to follow but we were first."

"As usual!" Howard says. "Alphas stay doing things first!"

"Of course I remember that as well." Darryl

Matthews jumps back in. That was indeed a crucial and pivotal time as it began a process for the fraternity that would lead us to where we are now.

"I'm glad that measures were put in place to help maintain the brotherhood for what it should be. A fraternity. Not a gang and not some sort of military force with unusual initiation tactics. We are a collection of college educated men who stand above academically." Jewel Callis states. "That sentiment, our sentiment, needs to be conveyed to each brother entering the House of Alpha."

"It's a topic that historically has been discussed over and over again." Brother Harris states. "It needed to be. Reform needed to happen, as someone stated, in all organizations. To ensure the longevity of our organizations, this dark side of it had to be dealt with."

"Let me ask a question pertaining to this and I don't want to be the odd man out but I gotta ask this." Howard takes the floor. "I'm not an advocate of hazing so let me say that first but I am about providing a way that brothers can come into the organization and truly respect it. I think we lost a lot by banning pledging and I'm not sure if it was worth it. I believe brothers can still be made right without all the brutality but still do some stuff."

"The problem with that Howard," Wil responds, "is the some stuff part. You have to define what can be done and what can't be done and brothers will always push the limits. If we in the national office came up with a plan and listed ten things that we came to conclude were proper to do, brothers would do eleven. That's reality. So since we know that's the case, we can't allow ten. We also can't wait for an incident to happen and then respond to it. We must put measures in place so that incident never happens."

"That's exactly right Brother Lyle." Jewel Murray states. "That's why it's reassuring to me that brothers such as yourself, Brother Johnson here, Brother Kagi out West, are in leadership positions in the fraternity. I respect your question Brother Franklin. It's a good question. I trust that Alpha men are smart enough to figure out a way to make newly initiated brothers feel welcome. At the same time, challenging them to own up to their oath and commitment. Yes there may be a fine line but there is a line that we can find. We have to show leadership in all levels of Alpha. Leadership in our regions, leadership in our districts and leadership in our chapters. That's who we are and that's who myself and these six gentlemen founded this organization to be. We made a decision to form a fraternity and to no longer exist as a social club. That means we wanted an aspect of brotherhood to exist. I believe we achieved that. Along with the good of the brotherhood came some of the ills of the secret society. That is what we have to purge out over time. I commend you brothers who serve in leadership positions who have made the necessary adjustments to ensure Alpha's future is guaranteed."

"Those are the things the brothers in the national office think about day in and day out. Our longevity and impact on our communities. Making sure Alpha is truly honoring what you seven men laid down for us in the beginning. No matter how much time passes, we have to make sure that your vision is what we are doing on the ground. Sound programs that will enhance the lives of you Black men and help to build our communities." Wil eloquently adds.

"Most of us in this meeting entered the House of Alpha during a time when pledging was above ground. Like Brother McCaskill shared, I'm two years removed as I came in a year before him and Brother Gourdine. When we came in, that's all we knew. It wasn't unusual at all to see a line of Sphinxmen or the Phi Beta Sigma Crescents running across the yard. I saw the Ivies of AKA and the Pyramids of Delta Sigma Theta Sorority. That was a very common sight back then. So it was indeed a little difficult making the transition. I agree like everyone else that it was a necessary transition. It had to be made. But it was strange to say the least. I wasn't sure at the time if the same brotherhood could be fostered if the same process didn't continue. I see now that it absolutely can but I definitely wasn't sure of that when this all went down between 1990 and 1991." Denny shares.

"Just know that your founders didn't envision that in the beginning. We first saw this as a means to strengthen the ties of Negro students who were widely separated on a White college campus. The great thing about the history of Alpha Phi Alpha is that the early vision was adjustable. By moving forward to Howard University, the same need wasn't present. Howard University never had Negro students in the minority in terms of campus population. All of the students were Black. So with the Beta Chapter being established, our vision for scholarship and love for mankind was embedded as well as the brotherhood of fraternity. That carried on and exists today. Never in that vision was the brutality that hazing turned into. We never wanted to beat a brother to be a brother. We never wanted to teach a lesson by beating the lesson into someone." This is the most passionate Jewel Murray has been in the town hall meeting. He continues. "I want every Alpha brother to recognize the value of this organization and what this fraternity means to each of us founders. When you act on behalf of Alpha Phi Alpha, you are representing a Jewel. You are representing Murray. You are representing Jones and Tandy. Callis and Chapman. Ogle and Kelley. You are representing the Jewels. You are representing the General President. You are representing your region, your chapter, yourself. You are wearing the letters that cause people to stop and say there goes an Alpha man. I want brothers to think about that each and every time they do anything in the name of Alpha Phi Alpha Fraternity. If it would bring embarrassment to you personally, don't do it. It would probably bring embarrassment to your founders. If it would have a negative impact on your chapter, don't do it. If it doesn't foster brotherhood, don't do it. Hazing has no place in Alpha Phi Alpha. It never has and never should have been introduced. Now that we have taken steps to move far from it, let's make sure we never allow these senseless acts to hinder our forward movement further."

"Well you said a mouthful Nate!" Jewel Tandy says laughing. A few brothers literally get up and exchange the fraternal handshake with Jewel Murray. He has said a mouthful and what he has shared is invaluable and timeless. The words he speaks were relevant when he spoke out against hazing years ago and applicable still today.

"Brothers, with that, why don't we take a short break? If you need to use the restroom or want to grab another bite, there's plenty of food left. Help yourselves and let's reconvene in the town hall meeting in 15 minutes." I think a break is in order as we have been talking back and forth since the meeting began. I'm sure every brother attending is enjoying this discussion as much as I am. This could probably continue for hours upon hours. I now understand when the Jewels often said that their debates and conversations continued through the wee hours of the morning, only to continue the following night. "The restroom is down th..."

"We know where the restroom is." Jewel Tandy shuts me up. That causes everyone to laugh as each brothers stands up and stretches.

As the brothers begin to disperse, some to the restroom and some to the table for food, Donald approaches me.

"Brother Gourdine, there's something I've really wanted to find out from Jewel Callis. I wonder if he doesn't mind answering it now."

"I'm sure he won't mind. Let's ask him." I say.

Donald and I approach Jewel Callis. He's standing by himself next to the table of food.

"Jewel Brother Callis. I'm wondering if you could clear something up for me. Something I've wanted to know for some time." Donald says.

"Sure. I hope I can be of assistance brother." Jewel Callis says with a smile.

"My question is regarding the original founders. Why was Wesley so dead set on there being seven original founders when there were actually eleven present when the fraternity was officially founded?" Donald asks.

Jewel Callis thinks before he speaks. "In coming up with the criteria for the status of a Jewel, a lot of factors were put into place. Mostly, the contribution of the members from the year of 1905 and the fall of 1906. After careful consideration, it was determined that the seven of us were deserving of the status while the others were listed as Alpha Chapter members. I assume your referring to Leumuel, Gordon and James."

"Yes sir. I also included Professor Poindexter."

"Why?" Jewel Callis asks although he probably knows the answer.

"Because Poindexter was still on the roll on December 4th. When the decision was made to become a fraternity on what we now know as Founders' Day, Poindexter's resignation wasn't received. So technically, he was still in the group."

"Not technically. He was still in the group." Jewel Callis adds. "Continue."

"So C.C. Poindexter was still there. His resignation wasn't accepted until January. So if you look at December 4th, you have yourself, Chapman, Jones, Kelley, Murray, Ogle, Tandy, then Lemuel Graves, Gordon Jones, James Morton and Professor Poindexter. That's eleven."

"I know some brothers have stated that we have seven Jewels and ten founders. They aren't including Professor Poindexter obviously because soon after we accepted his resignation."

"Indeed." Donald responds.

"But to answer your question, the decision for

seven was based on merit and contribution. The overwhelming majority felt that the seven chosen were most influential in the early days of the literary society and formation of Alpha Phi Alpha."

"And were you in agreement with that decision Brother Callis?"

Jewel Callis pauses before he answer Donald. "The overwhelming majority felt that the seven chosen were most influential in the early days of the literary society and formation of Alpha Phi Alpha." Jewel Callis smiles as if to say he has answered the question without answering the question. Donald and I smile as we get it. No more need be said regarding that.

I step away and approach Denny who is talking to Sean McCaskill. "You brothers doing alright?"

"Yes sir!" Sean says. "This is excellent man and you're doing a great job handling these questions!"

"Yeah Darrius, this is an incredible event. Hearing from the Jewels on these issues is outstanding." Denny cosigns. "Awesome is the only way I can describe it. The words from this town hall are going to live on in Alpha forever!"

"I certainly hope so. I want each and every brother to appreciate these guys the way you both do. I know both you guys and your love and passion for Alpha. I see it in your walk and I hear it when you share your Alpha story. All I want is for brothers to rekindle the fire inside. There was a time when each brother was so serious about the business of the fraternity. Usually right after they crossed. Then at some point along the way, life kicks in. Brothers get married or they get more responsibilities at work. Some have career changes or some genuinely lose interest. Whatever the reason, I want to find ways to close the back door so we lose no more brothers. That's what I would like to see as a result of interactions like this."

"That's what I was saying earlier. Falling in love with Alpha." Sean says. Brothers never forget the day they go over and the day they fall in love with Alpha. That fire may grow dim at times but it never goes out. We have to tap into that fire and make sure brothers can stay as on-fire for Alpha as they can so we can accomplish what we have to accomplish."

"Exactly right good brother!" Denny responds.

Some of the brothers make their way back to the main room. It hasn't been fifteen minutes but I'm sure the brothers are as anxious to get back to the discussion as I am. "Brothers if you need more time, we still have a few more minutes before we'll begin."

"I'm ready to get back into it!" Darryl says.

"Yeah man, let's go!" Howard cosigns.

"Fine with me. If everyone can take their seats, we can continue." I say. Everyone obliges and sits down where they were seated before.

"I have a question that is really specific to one person. Well two people I guess." Sean Gayle says.

"Okay go ahead."

"This is for Brother Wilson. You're the grandson of a Jewel. That has to be awesome! Can you share what it felt like to become a brother knowing that your grandfather is Jewel Robert Harold Ogle? And I guess Jewel Ogle you can maybe share what it feels like to have a grandson who is a brother."

"I would like to show respect to my elder and allow him to answer before I do." Julian says.

"That's perfectly fine." Sean says.

"I appreciate the gesture. Let me say this. I've always been big on family. I'm a family man. When I met Helen, I knew right away that she was the love of my life. She became everything I had ever wished and hoped for in a bride. When the good Lord decided to take her to heaven, I had to manage without her. No one ever took her place. I became father to two beautiful girls who grew to be lovely women. To now know that she gave birth to a man who is so distinguished and a brother of my fraternity is heartwarming and special. I hold Julian to the highest regard as a brother and my family. He is an accomplished individual. A true Alpha man. I can absolutely say that the image of a man worthy of the letters A Phi A across his chest that I envisioned back in 1906 is who Julian is now. I may be prouder to call him my grandson as he is to call his grandfather his Jewel."

Jewel Ogle's words have brought tears to Julian's eyes. I believe it is fair to say that every brother in the room is touched by Jewel Ogle's sentiments about his grandson. Of all of the expressions of brotherly love that have been displayed, this has been the most touching. We all have a connection to the seven Jewels through Alpha Phi Alpha but none of us are directly related to any of them. Julian Wilson stands alone in that category. I'm sure he's proud that he does.

"Thank you. That is very kind of you to say and I cannot adequately express how special your words are to me. Let me respond with this brothers." Brother

Wilson pauses and thinks before he continues. "To be an Alpha is a tremendous responsibility and undertaking. We should all take pride in these letters that we wear. What these men have laid out for us and what my grandfather has contributed to my life is extraordinary. The way my heart feels about Alpha at this stage is along the lines of how my grandfather and some of the other Jewels probably feel. I believe that we have great potential. I know we have great minds and great visionaries. I believe with the think tank that we are, there is no reason we aren't further along."

Uh oh, Brother Wilson is about to take us to church! I want to say that but I can't seem to open my mouth. The respect level is far too high for me to interrupt.

"I cannot sit here and say that I am disappointed in the fraternity because that isn't true either. We have accomplished so much. We have been giants in so many areas. At the same time, I don't see Alpha in the streets the way that I want to. Where are we? Why aren't we the lead in a political party? Why aren't we more present in the streets? I go feed the homeless with my chapter but then I go back by myself. Why? Because the homeless are still hungry the next day and the day after that and the day after that. I don't see brothers when I go back. I can't speak for all the founders but as for Jewel Ogle, my grandfather, I am so glad that we are connected by more than fraternity. I seem to have captured his spirit as I know how he feels about the state of Alpha. It's how we all probably feel. As great as it is, it can be better."

"You're right brother. You're absolutely right." Brother McCaskill says.

"Wow! That's all I can say. Just... wow!" Denny says.

"Yes brother, I agree. I'm speechless." Kagi comments.

"I have to echo these words." Jewel Jones adds. "My son became an Alpha and it warmed my heart. There's nothing like it in the world. To you brothers who have young boys you are raising up, steer them toward manly deeds. Both you and he will be satisfied that you did."

"Brothers, remember this moment. This is what Alpha Phi Alpha Fraternity is supposed to be about." Brother Harris says. What these seven gentlemen have created is resonating over 100 years later in this very meeting. If this isn't what fraternity is supposed to be about then I don't know what is."

"I agree wholeheartedly with you Brother Harris." Jewel Tandy says. "You have made a perfect assessment."

"I would just like to add that I respect and agree with your grandson Bob. It takes courage to be honest and I remember finding that courage when I saw Alpha go in directions that I didn't appreciate. I too feel that Alpha Phi Alpha should be doing more. Just as Brother Julian described. As appreciative as I am at how far we have come, I can only imagine how much further along we should be. Thank you for those words Brother Julian."

"You're welcome Jewel Kelley." Jewel Kelley shares some kind words and Julian is very appreciative. They are seated next to one another and Jewel Kelley puts his hand on Julian's shoulder.

"I have a question for the founders." Kagi says. His voice breaks an otherwise tense moment in which the brothers honestly face a reality that the Jewels may be pleased but not as pleased as they should be. We continue. "In the history book, it states that Jewel Henry Arthur Callis and Jewel George Biddle Kelley both worked in fraternity houses of White fraternities. At the time, Alpha Phi Alpha obviously wasn't established. Now that we are much more than established and it's been over 100 years, how does Alpha Phi Alpha Fraternity stack up against those fraternities now?"

"Let me find out the young bruh got a good question!" Howard says laughing. "Yes sir Brother Kagi! You aight with me bro! You aight with me!"

Everyone laughs.

"That is an excellent question brother and I wish I had more to contribute but I cannot say I am well versed in the affairs of Theta Beta Pi in current day." Jewel Kelley says. "I lost contact with those gentlemen and have not heard of their whereabouts. Not even certain of the status of the organization at this point."

"Thank you sir." Kagi says politely. "And you Brother Jewel Callis?"

"Sigma Alpha Epsilon is still alive and well. After all of these years, they are still here. They have chapters all over the country and still hold true to what their founders envisioned for their fraternity. I too have lost contact but I do see their accomplishments at times."

"How do they compare to Alpha Phi Alpha?"

"The irony is that there is no comparison in terms

of size. Sigma Alpha Epsilon has a little over 300 chapters. Alpha Phi Alpha has over 800. So we are almost 3 times their size which significantly increases our level of impact on our communities." Jewel Callis says.

"That is so interesting to me when I think about you working in their house on Cornell's campus. They were probably looking at Alpha in the early days as something that would never reach the level of success that they have and Alpha has more than surpassed it." Kagi says.

"What is even more ironic I think is the headlines that Sigma Alpha Epsilon has found itself in over the past few years." Sean McCaskill says.

"I was just about to comment on that." Donald says.

"They've had several racially charged allegations against them. One recently where an entire bus filled with their brothers sang a song with the word nigger in it. Someone recorded it with their phone and posted it to social media. Once that happens, of course it goes viral." Sean says. "And that isn't their only incident of a racial nature."

"You're right brother. They have had several recently. Maybe more that don't make the media spotlight." Donald adds.

"Did you encounter any negative racial interactions with any of their members back then? Either of you can answer." Kagi asks.

"I never received anything directly aimed at me or my comrades but the sentiment among the members and students in general was one of passive agreement.

It's as if White folks were doing us a favor by allowing us to matriculate at their university. In and of itself, that is a racist way of thinking. Not direct and outright in your face but very subtle." Jewel Kelley says.

"I saw a lot of it." Jewel Chapman adds. "Much of it was unspoken but very present on and off campus. We dealt with it though. I don't want to deviate from the original subject of the question however. I didn't work in any fraternity house so I cannot add to that part of the discussion."

"It's quite alright Jewel Chapman." I say. "This dialogue is open for anyone to chime in and discuss."

"Exactly. I appreciate your response too Jewel Chapman." Kagi says.

Jewel Murray chimes in. "People not familiar with the determined spirit that actuated your founders to continue to carry on, hurled verbal epithets at us such as 'You will be the laughing stock of the town!' 'You cannot hope to do what white folks do!' 'You are too poor and you have no money!' And the one that really caught my attention was when they said 'You will lose your jobs as waiters if you try to imitate your employer!' Or when they said 'You will go bankrupt after your first dance!' All of that was said to us on numerous occasions by many of them. Some fraternity members, some not. In either case, it was said and the sentiment was made known to all of us."

"And here we stand today successful, accomplished, well-educated and thriving. I think we did well!" Wil states.

"We did better than well! We excelled like only Alphas can!" Howard says enthusiastically.

"Even among the negative things that have been allegedly said about our people!" Denny adds.

"I know many of the men I was acquainted with at Cornell would be ashamed if these allegations of racist acts arose. I'm also very sure that many of the same members of their fraternity back then felt the same way as those expressing racist views." Jewel Callis continues with the topic.

"I just think there is so much irony in the fact that we have surpassed them in so many areas." Denny says.

"There is certainly irony there in that there was a time when I asked them for advice." Jewel Callis admits.

"Great question young brother." Brother Harris says with a smile.

"Thank you sir!" Kagi replies.

"Okay brothers, our next question is for all of the founders. If you could offer a word of advice to any young man considering membership in Alpha Phi Alpha Fraternity, what would you say to that young man?" I ask. This is a question I have been very interested in asking and I cannot wait to hear some of the responses.

"If you aren't willing to fight for this organization, then don't become a member of this organization." Jewel Tandy is first to answer. "I fought. We all fought. You can see the fight in our eyes. You can hear it in the passion of our speeches. If you don't fit that mold, then this may not be the fraternity for you. Alpha brothers are fighters. We don't take things lying down. We fight for what is right and what is right to us is manly deeds, scholarship and love for all mankind. If you're not willing to fight for these causes, then you are not a man worthy of Alpha Phi Alpha."

Both Howard and Greg stand and give Jewel Tandy an ovation. Brothers laugh as it is a comical gesture but his remarks are cosigned by everyone in attendance. He could've ended the town hall meeting on that very note. Not only were his words ringing true to each of us but the passion in which he said it ignited something in us as well.

"Yes Jewel Vertner! I couldn't agree with you more!" Howard excitedly exclaims. "That is the truth right there in a nutshell!"

"Yes sir that pretty much sums it all up!" Greg says.

Denny jokingly says, "I might need a cigarette after that one!" His statement causes everyone to laugh.

"Let me add to what my good brother Vertner stated. I want young men to know that we are not simply a fraternity for the sake of having a fraternity. You can find bonds of brotherhood in your own neighborhood on our own block. Alpha Phi Alpha Fraternity is a fraternity founded with the idea of service to others. If you are not already a service minded individual, then fraternity membership isn't for you and Alpha Phi Alpha definitely isn't for you." Jewel Jones adds to what Jewel Tandy has stated.

"I'd say this." Jewel Murray chimes in. "Do what you can by example, or by precept to encourage African American boys and girls of college grade, as well as those of high school, to carry the banner of racial achievement into places where it has never been waved, when placed in Black hands. Do this even though we as a group are in the minority or the majority. Believe in ourselves. Have a vision like Benjamin Banneker, Samuel Armstrong, Henry Ford, Booker T. Washington, Charles Wesley, Col. Lindbergh. Don't let anyone persuade you to change your goal. Keep your vision on your dream always ahead and work on and on."

"Great answer." Sean Gayle says.

"Thank you brother." Jewel Murray responds.

Jewel Callis speaks next. "I would tell a potential brother that what we need now is vision born of wisdom, for the next half century. Unencumbered citizenship requires unlimited responsibility."

"Well said Henry!" Jewel Tandy responds. "How about you Bob?"

"Let's see. What would I tell a young man interested in becoming a brother?" Jewel Ogle repeats the question out loud to himself. "I think I would look him in the eye and ask him what his beliefs are and where his convictions lie. Where does he stand in times of controversy or debate? Is he easily persuaded or does he stand firm in his conviction? Alpha men are leaders and not followers. I want to know where his mind is and where his heart will land him if he is challenged. The Alpha Phi Alpha that I founded sought men of caliber that could bring something to the fraternity. What can this young man do for Alpha Phi Alpha?"

"I remember when we selected and initiated Brother Giles." Jewel Callis speaks again.

"Roscoe C. Giles Sr. initiated into Alpha Chapter,

October 26, 1907." Donald says.

"That's exactly right! Now there was a brother who I considered to be Alpha material! He was an exceptional student and a good brother in general." Jewel Callis continues. "He absolutely added value to Alpha Chapter."

"He certainly did." Jewel Tandy cosigns.

"Brother Giles, became president of the chapter and the second General President of the fraternity! His contribution to Alpha Phi Alpha is without question. His merit and caliber was unprecedented." Jewel Callis adds.

"If I may," Brother Bob Harris says, "Brother Roscoe C. Giles Sr. approved the application for the formation of my beloved Theta Chapter. He holds a special place in my life and journey into Alpha Phi Alpha. What an extraordinaire man he was! He served as the president of Theta Chapter and a member of Xi Lambda Chapter in Chicago. He made his home there."

"That's right, he did." Jewel Callis responds. "I was always very proud of Roscoe as both a man and an Alpha man. He went into the same field of study as I did. He practiced medicine in Chicago for many years and was well respected."

"Roscoe C. Giles was the first African American to gain admittance into medical school at Cornell." Brother Harris says proudly.

"There goes an Alpha man!" Sean McCaskill announces.

"Wow, another first!" Kagi says.

"We need a list of accomplishments that Alphas are first at!" Howard says laughing.

"That would be a long list brother!" Gregory says.

"And Roscoe Giles would be at the top of that list! You ask what I would tell a young man who is earnest for the fellowship and brotherhood of Alpha Phi Alpha. I would tell him to approach the fraternal idea the same way Brother Roscoe did. He was anxious in his commitment. He didn't join our chapter and disappear, never to be heard from. He took leadership positions. He held leadership positions in every level in Alpha at that time. The young man who has desires of Alpha Phi Alpha today would want to be viewed as we brothers viewed brothers like Roscoe Giles."

"I'd like to share a quote that Brother General President Giles shared once. He said 'No more representative, no more intelligent, no more worthy men exist in fraternal bond in the world today than we boast of within our ranks.' This is one of the things I would share with a young man. Since Roscoe was mentioned, I think this quote is more than appropriate. I remember when we spoke with Roscoe about the concept of Alpha Phi Alpha and I remember the look in his eye. I would hope that each young man that brothers speak with would have the same look in their eye. Every potential brother who becomes a new brother ought to set his heart on being the caliber of brother as Brother General President Giles." Jewel Jones speaks fondly of the fraternity's second general president.

"Very well said of a great activist, surgeon, and General President!" Darryl Matthews says. "I'm honored to have served the fraternity in the same capacity as Brother Giles."

"Surprisingly, that brings me to my next question for the Jewels. Gentlemen, can you please tell us which General President you have admired the most over the years and why?" I ask. Immediately everyone starts shifting in their seats.

"Oh boy! This is gonna be good! This might get heated!" Howard says excitedly.

"Man that's a great question D!" Sean Gayle says.

"Yeah bruh, I can't wait to hear how this goes!" Denny responds.

"Well first of all," Jewel Kelley responds, "all of the answers should be George B. Kelley. So this should be the shortest question asked in this meeting." Everyone laughs loud as Jewel Kelley leans back and folds his arms as if he has said something monumental. Jewel Murray actually pats him on the shoulder as he is laughing.

"Yeah, you keep on believing that good brother!" Jewel Tandy says. Everyone laughs again.

"I don't know about the most admired President but I know the consensus on the least admired!" Gregory says. Everyone laughs but no one dares follow up on that statement. As the laughter diminishes, I step in to get us back on track.

"Jewel Kelley, since you spoke first, why don't you answer first?" I suggest.

"If you don't mind, I'd like to hear from some of my other brothers first." Jewel Kelley says. "I know who I would like to say but I'd rather not answer first.

"No problem. So, anyone is free to respond to the question. Your most admired General President and why." I say.

"I'll offer first then. My most admired General President is General President Charles H. Garvin. Brother Garvin was a physician, a civic leader which all Alphas should be and an extreme businessman." Jewel Ogle states.

"Which all Alphas should be!" Sean McCaskill declares.

"Amen brother!" Donald cosigns.

Jewel Ogle continues. "We were speaking of accomplishments earlier that were first done by Alpha men. General President Garvin was the first African American physician commissioned in the United States Army."

"Another first by an Alpha man!" Kagi says.

"Yes sir! And not only that, he was the first brother of Alpha Phi Alpha to publish historical information in The Sphinx magazine. As a matter of fact, he was the General President who pushed for the establishment of The Sphinx in the first place. Not only was he well established and invested in our beloved Alpha, but he also founded the Dunbar Life Insurance Company and helped organize Quincy Savings and Loan. He served as director and board chairman."

"Wow." Denny says.

"He was a member of many other worthy organizations. Too many to name but I will close with this. Another great Alpha accomplishment was the fact that he strongly encouraged his friend Garrett to become a member of the fraternity. Garrett did seek and obtain membership and they both served in the Pi Chapter of the fraternity in the Cleveland area. That is very significant as his friend Garrett is actually Brother Garrett Morgan who is the inventor of the modern day traffic light."

"One of his best known inventions." Brother Harris says. "He has several inventions under his belt but he's absolutely known for being the inventor of the traffic signal."

"All I can say is wow." Denny says.

"This is such a healthy and needed dialogue." Wil says.

"Brother Morgan, just to add one more Alpha first, is the first African American to own an automobile in the entire city of Cleveland." Jewel Ogle adds. "Now there goes an Alpha man!"

"I bet they said that when he drove by and they was all on the bus! There goes that Alpha man!" I say laughing. Everyone gets a good laugh out of that one.

"So I really admire President Garvin, not only for being the keeper of the record but for his contribution to Alpha and society in general." Jewel Ogle finishes.

"I'll pick up the baton now." Jewel Murray states. "For me it's an easy choice. General President Charles H. Wesley. I had the privilege of working with the General President when he worked on writing the history book. He and I had grown very close during that time and I definitely would select him as the General President that I most admire. I don't know if many brothers know this but it was Wesley that gave permanence to the term Jewel for your founders. The term was originated with Roscoe but it was Wesley that sealed it and made it permanent. I... we all, owe him an incredible debt for such a high honor in the fraternity. To be a founder in and of itself has its glorious upsides. To be given the designation of Jewel Founder adds so much in my mind. I love the term and appreciate Brother General President for seizing the opportunity to recognize your Jewels as such. I'm sure our Executive Director Brother Lyle knows a lot about Wesley after learning of your initiation chapter."

"Absolutely!" Wil responds. "Wesley was president of Wilberforce University and founded Central State University. Of course that's close to my heart and his legacy for those institutions is unmatched."

"I can talk about Wesley's accomplishments all day. He was one of the first five African Americans to receive a PhD from Harvard University. He holds degrees from Fisk University, Yale University, Harvard University and Wilberforce University. An accomplished scholar indeed as well as an ordained minister. Of course an author and a historian. He embodied the true spirit of the fraternity as he was a five term General President."

"Wow! Five terms?" Kagi asks.

"Yup!" Donald answers. "Wesley served five terms as GP."

"Yes. I admire this man greatly so to answer the question on the floor, this is exactly who I would recommend. The 14th General President, Brother Wesley." Jewel Murray finishes.

"Well I'm going to be a little more respectful and acknowledge the General President in the room. And no I'm not referring to George or Henry. I'm going to say I most admire Darryl Matthews." Jewel Tandy states.

"Why thank you kind sir!"

"Brother Matthews has an impressive resume to say the least! He walks upright and stately like an Alpha man should. He served as the Executive Director of the National Association of Black Journalists. That's the world's largest organization of Black journalists. He served as the Executive Director of the National Medical Association. He served as the Executive Director of Alpha Phi Alpha before he served the fraternity as its 32nd General President." Jewel Tandy proclaims. "Positions of leadership! Those are areas that we excel as Alpha men! In positions of leadership! We lead other men. We direct men. Perfect example of an Alpha Phi Alpha brother and a General President that I admire." Jewel Tandy has placed a humble smile on the face of Brother Matthews. "Tell them more about yourself brother! You sitting right here, speak for yourself! Don't let me mess it up!" Everyone laughs as Jewel Tandy suggests Brother Matthews continues.

"No brother Jewel, you did a fine job already."

"I know I must've missed something. What else you got brother?" Jewel Tandy insists.

"Jewel Tandy is a trip!" Howard says.

"I tried to tell you!" Donald responds laughing.

"Okay well, I'll just add this." Darryl agrees to continue about himself. "I helped engineer the passage of the legislation to construct the MLK Memorial. That legislation is called The King Bill. President Clinton signed it in 1996. That's what granted the fraternity the right to erect the memorial. I also served as Vice-Chairman of the board and as a member of the audit committee for the Memorial Foundation Project. So I'd close with that brothers. Thank you Jewel Tandy for your acknowledgement. It means so much to me for you to say that."

"No, thank you dear brother for your service. You are truly an Alpha man after my own heart and a great asset to this fraternity!" Jewel Tandy stands up and walks toward Darryl. Darryl stands and they exchange the fraternal handshake. What a moment this is. A definite highlight of the Town Hall Meeting.

"Thank you Jewel Tandy and Brother Matthews. Okay who's left?" I ask.

"I would have to say General President Raymond W. Cannon. I don't know how many brothers know this but the same year that General President Cannon appointed Brother Wesley to write the history book, he traveled to Florida. At the time, I was at Florida A&M University. He found me there and informed me that the brothers had lost contact with me and were inquiring about my whereabouts. Not only that, apparently the brothers thought I was deceased and listed me in Omega Chapter." Jewel Chapman shares.

"Really?" Sean Gayle asks.

"Yes. So President Cannon resurrected me if you will. I have to mention him of course." says the Jewel of few words.

"The General President that I admire the most is the one who was in office when I was designated a Jewel.

General President Antonio Maceo Smith was our 17th General President. I owe him gratitude. Many brothers may not know of his legacy and what he is responsible for in regard to our people. General President Smith was a great man! He dedicated his life in the fight for Civil Rights and never wavered. A true Alpha man! He fought against the White voting primary system in Texas which consistently disenfranchised non White voters. Due to his efforts, the Supreme Court decided in Smith vs Allwright to do away with White primaries nationwide! Now how many Alpha brothers today knew that an Alpha man was leading the way in that effort?"

"I wasn't aware of that at all!" I say.

"I didn't know that either." Sean McCaskill adds.

"I would suppose you could survey most brothers and they would not be aware of a fact like this. We ought to know the contributions of Alphas throughout the history of our country and mankind." Bob Harris says.

"That is a great bit of information. I wasn't aware of that either." Julian says.

"Jewel Brother Kelley. Are you prepared to share yet? I know you asked for a few moments to think about it." I ask.

"I believe I'm ready good brother. I would have to submit General President Ozell Sutton as the president I most admire."

"Oh that is a great choice!" Denny says.

"I concur." Bob Harris adds.

"Absolutely! Great choice!" Gregory states.

"Thank you." Jewel Kelley says. "I've always admired the work of Brother Sutton. I could see that he was destined for greatness. I admired him for his service to our country in World War II and for his dedicated work in Civil Rights. Many brothers may not know this but it was in 1996 that the White House decided on the land being approved for the Brother King monument. The fraternity voted on the monument in 1983 but didn't get the legislation signed until 1996. Brother Sutton was General President in 1983 so it was his administration that passed the fraternity legislation to honor Brother Dr. King. Here is the interesting part of the story brothers. In 1996, the meeting was held at the White House in order to secure the legislation. Brother Sutton and some of the other brothers were in that meeting. President Bill Clinton walked into the room and shouted 'Ozell!'

"Wow!" Howard says.

"President Clinton knew Brother Sutton from their days working together in government in Arkansas. You brothers did know that Ozell Sutton was from Arkansas." Jewel Kelley says.

"Yes! I happen to know that General President Sutton was from a town just outside of Gould, Arkansas. Then his family moved to Little Rock." Donald says.

"That is correct, brother historian. Did you all know that Brother Ozell was one of the first Blacks to serve in the United States Marine Corps?"

"Man, I never knew that of my brother." Kagi says.

"Don't feel bad brother. I didn't know that either

and I'm not sure any of us did." Denny says.

"I knew that." Gregory says. "But I know most brothers don't.'"

"Yes brothers, Brother Sutton should be a revered man in Alpha Phi Alpha. We all should esteem him well. He ought to be talked about with young brothers and reminisced with older brothers that knew him. His spirit needs to always live on within Alpha Phi Alpha. To the question asked of the caliber of a good Alpha man, he is the blueprint. Ozell Sutton."

"Well said." Wil says. "He absolutely was an extraordinaire man and leader. A well respected man in plenty of circles."

"He marched with Brother Dr. King in 1963 in the March on Washington and in 1965 in Selma. He worked in the Arkansas State Government as the Director of the Governor's Council on Human Resources. He was the founding member of the executive board of the National Center for Missing and Exploited Children. When Brother Sutton was GP, he was named one of the 100 most influential Black Americans by Ebony magazine." Jewel Kelley brags.

"A magazine owned and operated by an Alpha man!" Sean McCaskill says. "Brother John H. Johnson!"

"Such an extraordinaire brotherhood. So much potential to do so much. Glad to hear of all of the accomplishments of the brothers." Julian says.

"Yes indeed." Jewel Kelley continues. "Brother Sutton was honored by President Barack Obama for being among the first Blacks to serve in the Marines. He was given the Congressional Gold Medal by

President Obama. It's one of the two highest civilian awards in the country."

"What is the other highest award?" Kagi asks.

"The Presidential Medal of Freedom." Donald answers.

"That's exactly right. The Congressional Gold Medal that Brother General President Sutton received is awarded to persons who have performed and achievement that has an impact on American history and culture recognized in the recipient's field. So because he was outstanding in what he did, he was awarded the medal. A true accomplishment in life!"

"There goes another Alpha man!" Jewel Tandy declares.

"Excellent analysis Jewel Kelley!" Brother Harris says. "Truly excellent analysis!"

"I'm glad you took a moment to think about it." Sean Gayle says.

"Thank you brothers." Jewel Kelley responds with a smile.

"I will finish this question up with General President Moses Morrison. I served General President Morrison as his Vice President and was honored to do so." Jewel Callis states. "There are a few things I would like to say about this brother. Most of you probably know that he is Alpha Phi Alpha's first General President. That fact is commonly known among Alpha brothers for it is taught as a part of the history. I'm sure Brother Gourdine and Brother Gayle are aware that Brother Morrison was initiated at Beta Chapter. You are all probably aware of that fact."

"I believe every brothers knows that." Sean Gayle says.

"They better!" I say jokingly. Everyone laughs.

"If not, we can blame Beta." Jewel Tandy says with a smile and a nod toward Sean.

"I don't know if every brother knows that General President Morrison is one of only five general presidents who served as GP during their college days. He was of course at Howard at Beta Chapter. Roscoe was at Cornell with us at Alpha Chapter. Then there was Brother Frederick Miller at Epsilon Chapter at the University of Michigan. Brother Charles Garvin who was also at Howard University and Henry Lake Dickason who was at Ohio State University at Kappa Chapter. These five brothers are the only brothers who will obviously ever hold this unique distinction. General President while being a college brother!"

"You got that right!" Howard says laughing. "That'll never happen again!"

"General President Morrison's work was admiral to say the least! It was under his administration that Alpha expanded from four chapters to seven chapters. I'm sure my Jewel brothers remember how important our early expansion was to us. That sentiment was important to Moses too. Epsilon, Zeta and Eta Chapters were formed during his time as President. Let me share this as well. How many of you knew that every member of Brother Morrison's administration served as General President?"

"Really?" Sean Gayle asks.

"That is absolutely incredible!" Denny says.

"That is the truest essence of leadership." Sean McCaskill adds. "You can tell the caliber and quality of any good leader by the leaders he raises up. The mere fact that every one of his administrators became General President says a lot about Moses Alvin Morrison. We as Alpha men and as leaders ought to strive to do the exact same thing. We should be striving to bring out the best in those that are under our command. If we are mentoring someone, we need to impart in them our wisdom and understanding so they can do the same. Leaders create leaders! Leaders replicate themselves!"

"Man that is awesome Jewel Callis. Thank you for sharing." I say.

"You're welcome." Jewel Callis replies.

"Who were all those brothers if you know?" Gregory asks. "The brothers from his administration."

"Let me see if I can answer that." Donald says. "Simeon S. Booker served as Secretary. Roscoe Conklin Giles was the Treasurer. As mentioned, Jewel Callis was Vice President."

"Well done Brother Ross!" Jewel Callis commends Donald on his correct answer.

I stand and address the brotherhood. "Alright brothers! All of the Jewel Founders have answered and we definitely appreciate them for their responses to that question. I, for one, have been enlightened by being here and I want to take this time to thank each of the Jewels for their responses." I begin my closing.

Each of the brothers begins to applaud the founders. The founders clap for themselves as well. This has been an incredible discussion and time of sharing. The valued history of Alpha Phi Alpha ought to be always passed down so that new leadership understands legacy. As we build Alpha to serve the needs of our communities and our brothers, we cannot forget the shoulders we stand on or the spirit of brotherhood among us.

"I would like to extend an invitation for closing remarks from each of the Jewels if you choose to do so. You have the floor. Thank you once again for what you created." I take my seat.

"Some of them are preachers so we better give them a two minute time limit!" Donald says joking. Everyone laughs.

"Hmmmm... will the church say, amen!"

"Amen!" Everyone responds in unison at Jewel Tandy who mimics the voice of a Southern Baptist minister.

"I guess I'll go first then!" Jewel Tandy stands. "Brothers of Alpha Phi Alpha! We need to fortify our defenses and gird ourselves to the larger significance of our standards. We must put aside the precocity of the imitative social snob and undertake the challenge of our social responsibilities, both to ourselves and to the masses of our people of common experience and of common estate. Then the ideas of our vision shall have been fulfilled. We shall continue to be and to become, in act as well as in mind, the first Ethiopian brotherhood, the buttress of our troubled people and an outstanding force in a world of change. We shall be not a dead and imitative tradition, but a democratic living culture. Thank you for this opportunity and thank you for who you are in Alpha Phi Alpha." Jewel

Tandy takes his seat. The brothers applaud him.

There is a moment of silence in the room in which the Jewels look at one another as to who should speak next.

"It has been an honor and a privilege to meet each of you. Thank you." Jewel Chapman pauses. "Regardless of the many, many purposes each of us may devise as the activating principle in our life and the many goals toward which we may be striving, I can see, nevertheless, that we do have one supreme purpose for our existence as a fraternity, and that is the recognition, as well as the development and thereby the making of better men. You can realize that. Brothers... this can be only accomplished by the raising and elevating the lives of other people. God bless you as you endeavor to do just that."

As each Jewel founder makes his final remarks in this Town Hall Meeting, it reminds each of us of words of wisdom we all received as newly initiated brothers of Alpha. Whether it was a dean, an Alpha mentor or a sponsor, someone spoke encouraging words into us. Whoever it was and whenever it was, those words held fast and helped us all to embrace the spirit of brotherhood that we all cling to now. For me personally, it was my dean Jaret C. Riddick and our chapter advisor Leroy Lowery. In his own right, an Alpha among Alphas. Brother Lowery is the son of another great Alpha man, Brother Joseph Lowery. Brother Joseph Lowery was the third president of the Southern Christian Leadership Conference. He became president after Brother Martin Luther King Jr. and before Rev. Ralph Abernathy. He was at the forefront of most of the major civil rights campaigns in the 1960's. His son, Leroy served the fraternity as

Eastern Region Vice President, the office that Sean McCaskill held. He also served with the Martin Luther King Memorial Foundation. A well respected brother and I was honored to have him as my chapter advisor when I was initiated in 1990. I'm sure every brother in this meeting can give accolades to the brother that spoke words into them as I do of Brother Lowery.

Jewel Callis is next to stand. He takes his time in standing and takes his time in beginning his closing remarks. "Brothers, we students breathed the ideals of Ezra Cornell whose brainchild it was to regard the university as a seat of learning for anyone who desired a college education. Since its founding in 1906, Alpha Phi Alpha has recognized its responsibilities and has nurtured a leadership to aid the Negro in is struggle toward unfettered American citizenship. Education for intelligent participation in American life has been the tocsin. I wish to share this however, in light of this meeting being one of positivity and uplift. My sincere concern brothers, is that I am not certain we are prepared for the responsibilities of this period. Our interests have become too narrow. Dances and cocktail parties replace discussion of current problems and active participation in community and regional affairs." He pauses before he continues. Each of the brothers is glued to his every word. "In 1906, three thousand lynchings had occurred in a quarter-century. Disfranchisement was law in one third of the states. Separate but unequal had become an entrenched practice throughout the nation. The Niagara Manifesto, demanding full rights under the constitution for all Americans, was heresy. What are the dangers ahead in the next half century? They are not new. Success and prosperity breed selfishness and indifference. These vices undermine the fire society that spawns them. Eternal vigilance remains still the price of liberty. Freedom for one's self cannot be divorced from responsibility for one's fellow."

"Preach!" Sean McCaskill calls out as if we're in church.

"Say that again Jewel Callis!" Howard encourages.

"Freedom for one's self cannot be divorced from responsibility for one's fellow. Nor is freedom divisible. There is not one freedom for thought, another for speaking, another for reading, another for association and yet another for travel. As citizens, our obligation is to guard jealously, the complete freedom for all Americans. Only this vigilance will keep America strong and keep us free. Every brother should take pride and feel a corresponding responsibility in the historic fact that Alpha Phi Alpha is the first Greek letter college fraternity founded with social purpose. Young brothers seldom fail to catch the vision; let the Brothers who, like the Founders, have reached fifty, keep the vision. What we need now is vision born of wisdom, for the next half century. Unencumbered citizenship requires unlimited responsibility. The chief significance of Alpha Phi Alpha lies in its purpose to stimulate, develop, and cement an intelligent, trained leadership in the unending fight for freedom, equality and fraternity. Our task is endless. Thank you."

As Jewel Callis takes his seat, not only do brothers applaud him for his words but they stand as they applaud. Jewel Ogle, Jewel Murray and Jewel Tandy stand as well. Jewel Chapman pats him on the back.

"Great sermon Pastor Callis!" Jewel Tandy says as he takes his seat.

The room comes to order and Jewel Nathaniel Murray stands. "Not sure how I'm going to follow that but I'll give it my best. I remember the early days. As was to be expected, some opposed and some favored the new proposition. After drifting along for several weeks with no definite decision forthcoming, I offered the motion that I believed the time was ripe to disband the social club and organize a Negro College fraternity. Did we have fights? Yes, but only verbal fights. Did we call names, only to be balled out by the chairman. Did we have personal grievances? Yes, yet despite personal grievances, we put Alpha Phi Alpha first and when the time came to go home at the hours indicated, we all gave the good hand of fellowship and left ready to resume the battle the next night, or the next called meeting. I encourage you all to do the same and be the same. For dear A Phi A."

Jewel Kelley is next. "I said to a man who stood at the gate of the year, 'Give me a light that I may tread safely into the unknown,' and he replied, 'Go out into the darkness and put your hand into the hand of God. That shall be to you better than a light and safer than a known way.' Such a thought must have been in the mind of each founder over one century ago. A century is such a long span for the life of an organization such as ours that one cannot but thank the Almighty who has shaped its existence. We have nurtured our little plant from its beginning with brotherly love and the water of human kindness. We have not come to our present growth through the efforts only of the Founders and our changing General Officers. We have grown because the various brothers from the dates of their initiation have nurtured the plan. I cannot close without giving thanks and credit to the Black people of Ithaca who so kindly aided us in our years at Cornell and encouraged us in the formation of our fraternity. Together, with Mother Singleton, they were large in number. As a founder who cherishes his part in the formation of the fraternity, I thank all of the brothers who make Alpha Phi Alpha Fraternity what it has become. Thank you."

As Jewel Kelley sits, Jewel Ogle stands. "Founded on a platform of service, loyalty and reverence to God and our fellow brothers," Jewel Ogle begins, "we have learned that the greatness of any group of men lies not in the fine buildings they erect, or the numerous air castles planned but never erected, but rather in service to God and your fellow brothers. That service is performed whether it can be in the fraternity house, on the street, on the school campus, at a public gathering, or in your own home. We are familiar with the resplendent record of achievement marking the rapid growth of Alpha Phi Alpha in numbers and power. We know that its fundamental principles are true and strong. We believe that the men of the college world and other citizens of the United States see it in the embodiment of all that is noble in African American manhood. Alpha Phi Alpha undoubtedly faces the most challenging test in its history. It is of vital importance that we seriously consider the contribution every brother may make for the good of our fraternity."

Jewel Jones begins to speak without standing. He is the only one who has chosen to make his final remark without standing. "I thank each and every one of you, my brothers, for this dialogue. As you are well aware, my passion is the uplift of our race, race relations and the longevity of our brotherhood." He continues. He speaks as if he is addressing an arena filled with thousands as was his common practice. Today his audience is 18 fraternity brothers hearing his words and thousands of fraternity brothers listening to his heart. "The Negro has been considered the most easily understood of racial groups because of his frank, open face, jovial nature and his extraordinary ability to pantomime to give expressions to his thoughts. The White race and the Negro race in America are each possessed of heritages and have had racial experience so vastly different. They are given an unusual opportunity to prove the possibilities of a true democracy where different races of mankind may live in peace and harmony, each one giving of his best to the welfare of all and to the glory of God and man. The Negro brought in as a slave was not introduced into the economic life of the country as a competitor to the White man, but as an aid. I doubt whether any statesman of the periods in which Negroes were brought to America as slaves would have continued the experiment if they had known that 1865 would have recorded on American soil Negroes to the number of four million, eventually to become industrial competitors to White men. This is where we as Alpha men can and will excel. Success in American life is fraught with competition. African Americans today must compete not only with members of other races, but with those within our own race who have caught the vision of the new age and who are lured along by the attraction of success. The rank and file are dependent upon trained men and women for guidance and extraordinary service. Be those trained men my Alpha brothers. For you are equipped to succeed! Be the voice of guidance! For you are the educated and have been well prepared to advise and guide! Lastly, provide service to all mankind! For you are Alpha Phi Alpha brothers and must always strive to be the agents of extraordinary service! A Phi!"

"Oh six!"

Nearly everyone in the room responds boldly. A fitting conclusion to The Town Hall Meeting.

# Thank You

Thank you Lord for gifting me with the ability to write. I promise You that I will honor you by writing all the days of my life. Thank you to my wife Kathy and my son Dylan in whom I continually write for. Thank you to the brothers of Alpha Phi Alpha Fraternity Incorporated who continue to support my work. I appreciate all of your words of encouragement regarding my books and for your follows on social media. This fraternity means the world to me and I appreciate the continuous support of my brothers. Thank you to the 11 brothers who agreed to be a part of this project. Brother General President Darryl R. Matthews Sr., Brother Robert L. Harris, Brother William Douglass Lyle, Brother Denny N. Johnson, Brother Sean McCaskill, Brother Donald Ross, Brother Kagi Kananga, Brother Sean Christopher Gayle, Brother Gregory Parks, Brother Howard Franklin and Brother Julian Wilson. There are no words to adequately express my gratitude for what you brothers have contributed to this book. Thank you from the bottom of my heart. Each of you agreed to be a part of this without hesitation and lent your voice and input. I thank you! Thank you to Brother Jossan Robinson for the awesome book cover and promo designs. Thank you to Norman Rich for the book layout and website maintenance. Thank you to James McDuff for my photo shoot for the back cover. A big thank you to all of my fans of As the Sands Burn over the years. It's because of all of your emails and words of encouragement that I continue to write.

Lastly, thank you to the person holding this book and reading it right now. I hope you have been blessed by this enactment of a Town Hall Meeting. As you close this book, remember one thing from the lives of the Seven Jewels... if God could do it for them, He can do it for you and I as well!

God bless you richly and mightily!

Darrius Jerome Gourdine

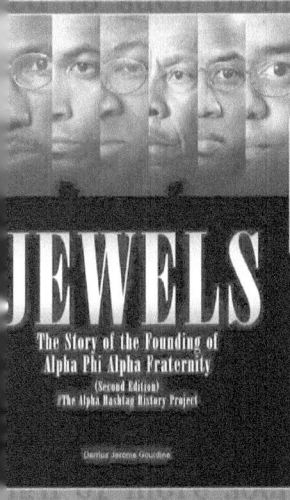
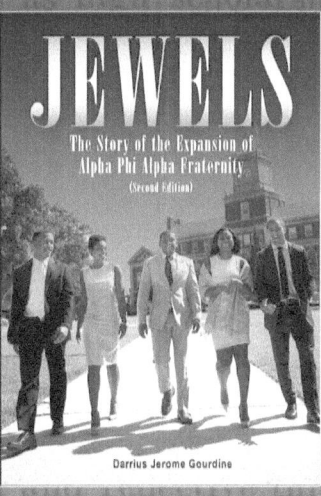

www.ingramcontent.com/pod-product-compliance
Lightning Source LLC
Chambersburg PA
CBHW030330020726
47493CB00004B/1225